CLAIRE RAYNER

LADY MISLAID

PIATKUS

Copyright © Claire Rayner 1968

This first hardcover edition published in 1982 by Judy Piatkus (Publishers) Limited
of Loughton, Essex

ISBN 0 86188 136 2

Printed in Great Britain by
The Garden City Press Limited
Pixmore Avenue, Letchworth, Hertfordshire SG6 1JS

LADY MISLAID

CHAPTER ONE

It had been years since she played this game with herself. She lay still, cocooned in the warmth of her bed, holding back the moment when awareness would come to flood her with thoughts of the day to come, memories of the yesterday now lost in the past. She had been able as a child to lie suspended in time in the orange coloured blankness behind her closed lids, knowing that the morning sun was shining, but not knowing where she was, or why she was, even who she was. And she could still do it.

But outside things began to creep in, as they always used to. There were birds singing somewhere, quite near. And the windows must be open wide, because there was a smell of lilac and fresh cut grass.

Lilac. Lilac? She let thought spread wider. Why a smell of lilac? There wasn't any lilac—

And then a sound cut across, a knock at a door, and her eyes snapped open, to stare round at the room in which her bed was. A pretty room, with flowered wallpaper and sprigged cotton curtains stirring at an open window, but with a certain impersonal quality about it. The only evidence of occupation were some clothes lying across a chair, and an open suitcase and a brown leather handbag on the otherwise empty dressing table.

The tap came again, and automatically, she called 'Come in—'. A young woman in the neat white coat of a servant pushed open the door, a tray balanced on one hand. 'Good morning, Mrs. Miles,' she said brightly. 'A lovely morning, isn't it? Your tea and paper. I hope you slept well?'

She put the tray down on the little table beside the bed, and the girl in it lay and stared at her, blankly. And the white coated woman nodded at her, put the newspaper on the pillow and went away, closing the door quietly behind her.

The girl in the bed sat up, and shook her head with sudden irritation. The time for the game was over now. Her eyes were open, so it was time for the thought of the day to come, the memories of yesterday—

But they didn't come. Awareness was there, but no memory. The pretty impersonal room was completely strange. The smell of lilac was completely strange. *Everything* was completely strange. And what had the woman in the white coat said? 'Good morning, Mrs. Miles—'

But I'm not Mrs. anybody, the girl in the bed thought wildly. I'm Abigail Lansdon, and I'm not married! She looked round at the room again, and moved sharply, swinging her legs over the side of the bed. The newspaper on the pillow slithered to the floor, and automatically, she bent to pick it up. It was folded so that the date showed clearly. Tuesday, the ninth of May, she read almost without thinking. The ninth of May – 1967.

'But this is *mad*—' she said aloud. 'Mad— Next week is my birthday – next week.' She clung to this memory gratefully. 'Next week on the eighteenth of May I'll be twenty-one' – she began to do sums in her head. 'I was born in nineteen forty-five. Just at the end of the war. Right?' Right, her mind answered. 'Which means that next week, when it's my birthday, it will be nineteen sixty-six. But the paper says May, nineteen sixty-seven. So what on earth is going on?'

For a sickening moment, the room seemed to swirl around her, so that she leaned back again against the pillows. '*Think*,' she murmured aloud, 'Think properly—'

Remember your training, Nurse Lansdon, and be logical. Start at the beginning. You have just finished your State Registration course. Next week – after your birthday – you'll be admitted to the Register. I mean, you *were* admitted to the Register once you were twenty-one, and when was that? Anyway, you've had a good nursing training, so *think*. What does it mean? If this newspaper is right, and there is no logical reason why it should not be, you are now in nineteen sixty-seven – so you've lost a year somewhere. Which is ridiculous, because people don't go around mislaying chunks of the calendar in this foolish fashion. So, there must be something wrong with *you*, and not the calendar.

She opened her eyes again, and the tea tray beside her seemed to offer something real to hold onto in an unreal world. The tea tasted good, hot and fragrant, and she sipped it gratefully, staring unseeingly over the edge of the cup as she went on trying to put her thoughts into some sort of reasonable order.

All right. You are the out-of-gear one, not the paper and its date, so, what are the possibilities?

Amnesia, came the prompt reply, as prompt as an answer to an examination question. And then she laughed, almost spluttering over her tea.

Amnesia – that's silly. It doesn't happen to people just like that – does it? Types of amnesia, her mind said busily, collecting facts from the store house her training had built up. Retrograde, following head injuries. Hysterical, due to intense emotional stress, with which the patient is unable to cope. Malingered amnesia, very useful for people in trouble, but which doesn't really work when they meet a good psychiatrist—

Well, this certainly isn't malingered, she told herself with wry amusement. Retrograde? Possibly. Hysterical? I don't *feel* very hysterical. A bit scared, maybe. Worried, but not all that much. And anyway, what emotional stress have I had lately to trigger off that sort of amnesia?

Ass, her mind retorted. If you could remember that, you wouldn't be amnesic, would you? That's the whole point of this sort of amnesia – to forget the stress that caused it.

Be practical, she told herself firmly. Practical. So you've got amnesia of some kind or another, which is a laugh of a sick sort, but sitting here laughing won't get you anywhere. Get yourself going, Abigail Lansdon, and go look for your lost memory. End of problem.

'But it isn't—' she spoke aloud again. Of course it isn't, the voice in her mind retorted. But it's as far as you can go with it at the moment. So get *going*.

Now I know what they mean in books when they talk about people doing things in a dream, she thought, getting out of bed. I'm in a dreamlike state too, cleaning my teeth, washing, dressing, all in a dream.

The clothes lying on the chair, obviously once worn, were undoubtedly hers. They fitted her so well – and the girdle and bra and stockings still held some of her own shape in their fabric. But they were so much nicer, so much more expensive than anything she'd ever worn before. The underwear, lacy and good, the neat tweed skirt, the soft cashmere sweater in exactly the same honey colour as the tweed, the brownish suede shoes with their neat stacked polished wood heels. There was expensive makeup in the handbag on the dressing table and hopefully, she rummaged through the bag for some evidence of her ownership of it. But all there was was the makeup, a small wallet holding twenty-five pounds in crisp new notes (at least I'm not broke, she thought) and some loose change, a handkerchief, and a Yale key on a ring. A most impersonal collection.

She looked at the suitcase, then. There were more good

clothes – a dress made of a silky green fabric, a suit in crisp black barathea, a white guipure lace blouse, a change of underwear. Very lush, she thought approvingly. Just what I'd choose myself if I could afford it. And then she laughed again. I probably did choose them!

There was a watch lying on the dressing table, too, a small gold one on a black ribbon bracelet, and hesitantly, she put it on. Why not? It must be mine, after all. And then, for the first time, she noticed her own hands, her left hand in particular, as she fastened the watch on her wrist. A wedding ring, a broad smooth gold band, circled her fourth finger.

She stared at it, her own pinkly varnished nails, longer than she usually wore them, and the sense of strangeness that had hovered around her from the moment she first woke suddenly overwhelmed her in great waves of panic. My hand – no, her hand – a hand, somebody's hand, *whose* hand?

It took every scrap of will she had to make herself stop shaking, to bring back the mood of cool calm common sense her thinking had created. But bring it back she had to, if she wasn't to run screaming with fear from this cruelly sunshiny beflowered room. And screaming never helped anyone—

It was almost as though she were a member of an audience watching a play at the same time as being one of the actors on the stage. She watched herself brush her hair. That was the same, anyway, still hanging in smooth leaf-brown curtains beside her narrow fair skinned face, still cut in a square fringe above her long amber coloured eyes. Watched herself put lipstick on her pale mouth and then walk to the door beyond which lay – what?

And then she stopped being audience, and became just the bewildered actor, moving hesitantly in an unrehearsed

11

play, improvising as she went along. The Method, she thought, and giggled. This is a hell of a time to start thinking about methods of acting, for pity's sake!

Outside there was a wide corridor, lined with doors, each of which had a number on it. At the far end there was the start of a flight of stairs, and she stood hesitantly outside her own door, her head up, trying to take in all the information she could.

A nurses' home, like the one at the Royal where she had trained? No – it doesn't feel right for that. And the smells – they weren't right for a nurses' home either. She lifted her head, almost like a hunting dog sniffing the wind. Floor polish – yes, that was nurses' homeish. So was the faint smell of soap and talcum powder, that hint of bathrooms. But there were other smells. Cooking. Bacon. Coffee. They'd be right for a nurses' home, but what was the other odour that made it feel so foreign? And then she knew what it was. The smell of relaxation, of parties. Cigar smoke and cocktails, gin and potato crisps, and, well, *parties*.

Suddenly, it all clicked into place, the numbered doors, the white coated woman who had brought the tea, the smell of gin and tobacco. An hotel. A small hotel – no chrome here, no lifts, no air of discreet richness. A country hotel – those singing birds and lilac and new-cut grass outside the bedroom window.

She felt enormously elated suddenly, as though she had been doing a very difficult crossword puzzle, and the most complicated clue had yielded up its answer. There was *fun* in this mad situation, the fun of finding the clues, and then solving them. At this rate, she'd have all the answers in no time.

Her optimism carried her forwards almost gaily, to the staircase and halfway down it. And then she stopped again.

Below her, in the square hallway, was the evidence that her deduction was right. A reception desk, a notice board, a rack of keys, another of letters. A porter in a short white jacket, rubbing lackadaisically at the brass knob on the wide open door. A swathe of sunlit cobblestones beyond.

She became aware of two other figures. There was a big dark man, with his back to her, staring at the notice board with its litter of coloured posters. And another man, also dark but slighter in build, standing behind the desk, his head bent over some papers. She stared hard at them both, hoping to find in the way they looked some other clue to this mad situation, but they offered no triggers to her memory at all.

Almost as though he felt her eyes on him, the man at the desk looked up, smiled widely, showing his lower teeth as well as his upper ones, in a curiously false bonhomie. The manager, her mind said at once, and she felt a lift of elation again. Clues, clues, more of them!

'Good morning, Mrs. Miles!' the manager said loudly, yet with a sort of caressing softness in his voice that she found rather unpleasant. 'I hope you were quite comfortable last night?'

'Er – yes, thank you,' she said, and began to move again, towards the bottom of the stairs. She felt rather than saw the big man at the notice board turn round sharply and look at her.

'Good!' the manager said, filling the word with an enthusiasm that was very overdone. If I'd said the place was like Buckingham Palace he could hardly sound more gratified, Abigail thought rather irritably.

'Well, I hope your whole stay with us will be just as comfortable! We'll certainly do our very best to make it so!' He bustled towards her, and smiled his disagreeable smile again. 'And if there is anything I can do –

personally, – his voice dropped to a confidential level – 'just say the word. I'd be more than delighted to show so charming a guest around the many lovely beauty spots we have here – more than delighted. Indeed, if I may say so, the company of so – *attractive* a lady as yourself would make my lot a very happy one indeed.'

Her flesh crawled, almost, so sleek did the man look and sound. They say women staying alone in hotels get passes made at them, she thought, irritable again. They aren't joking.

She opened her mouth to say something that would, without sounding too unpleasant, make it clear that she didn't want the manager's personal attentions, and caught the eye of the man by the notice board, now leaning against it with his hands in his pockets, staring unashamedly at her. And the look of – what was it – scorn – yes, scorn, on his face made her flush suddenly, made her speak more sharply than she had meant to.

'That won't be necessary, thank you,' and with her head up, she marched past the manager, who had stepped back, towards the door.

'Well, just say the word—' the manager said, recovering from this rebuff, and following her. 'In the meantime, where will you take breakfast? Here in the dining room' – one hand pointed vaguely towards the left hand side of the hallway – 'or on the terrace?'

'The dining room will do very well, thank you,' Abigail said, and a little ashamed of her irritability, smiled at the manager who, smirking a little, promptly held the dining room door open for her. Without turning round, she knew the big man had followed her, was still staring at her, and annoyed and embarrassed turned what she knew was a beaming smile on the manager. I'll give that great staring idiot something *to* stare at, she thought unreasonably, and let the manager settle her at a table with much flurrying of table napkins and beckoning of waiters.

The big man sat down at a table directly opposite her, and for the first time dropped his eyes from their steady stare at her, reading the menu card propped up before him.

The manager was still bustling about her, but now more than anything she wanted to get rid of him, to have time to think again. So, when he offered her a newspaper, she accepted it gratefully, and opened it purposefully. And to her relief, the manager took the hint, and went away.

She ordered coffee and toast and marmalade, and while she waited for it, began to read the paper in earnest. Maybe there would be something there that would give her another precious clue to solve, some account of – what?—Earthquakes, fires, road accidents – anything that might explain why she found herself in a strange hotel, in an unknown place, a year later than it ought to be.

Doggedly she read the paper from front to back. No earthquakes. No fires. Nothing that could offer any clues at all. There was one story, however, that did make her feel a sudden pricking of tears behind her lids, but even as she read it, she knew why it made her feel that way. And she also discovered that her memory was intact up until that time a week before her twenty-first birthday, which was one comfort. Cold comfort, but better than nothing.

It was odd, like one of those very futuristic films which jump about in time. Here she was reading a newspaper story, while unrolling in her mind was the story of a very much younger Abigail, a girl who had been bitterly unhappy.

'The police are seeking a woman whom it is hoped will

help them with investigations into the disappearance of nine year old Daniel Tenterden, her stepson.'

A stepmother, Abigail remembered, and felt again the aching frustration of trying to love a woman who didn't like her, didn't want her—

'—foul play is suspected,' she read, 'since a heavy implement, on which were found traces of blood and hair, was found in the woman's home—'

The times I wanted to hit *her* till she was dead, cried young Abigail, deep inside the mind of adult Abigail. The way I hated her —

'—the boy's father has returned from a stay abroad to help police in their investigations into his son's whereabouts, and it is hoped he will be able to assist them find his also missing wife—'

If she hadn't turned up, Daddy wouldn't have died, young Abigail wept, beating helplessly behind the eyes of grown-up reading Abigail, making tears blur the print. If only he'd been able to come back to help me, but he never did, he never did. He was dead, poor, poor man, he was dead. Poor, poor Abigail—

Her hands shaking a little, Abigail put down the paper, and made herself eat some of the crisp toast, drink the black sweet coffee. It's been a long time since I remembered, she thought bleakly. A long time. Her father's death, just a few weeks after his second marriage. Her resentment of the woman who so patently found her a drag and a bore. Her utter conviction that it was the marriage that had hastened his death – unjust as she now knew, but so deeply ingrained in her that she would never really rid herself of it.

But – and resolutely, Abigail pulled herself back into the very real present – at least I know who I *was*. And that means who I still *am*. They can call me Mrs. Miles till they're blue, but it doesn't alter facts. I'm Abigail

Lansdon. I must be, or I wouldn't remember so much about being me, would I?

The childishness of the logic made her smile suddenly, and aware again of the man at the opposite table, she put her hand up to her mouth to hide the quirk of her lips. And saw again that wedding ring.

Covertly, she rested her hand again on the table, and looked more closely. Gently, she moved the ring down her finger, twisting it to make it slip over the skin, for it was rather tight. And saw very clearly the white mark where it had rested. The rest of her hand was lightly tanned, but there, encircling that fourth finger, a white mark —

I've worn it – how long? she asked herself miserably. You don't get a mark like that in five minutes, do you? *Am* I Mrs. Miles? Or Nurse Lansdon? She rolled the name around her mind, tasting it. Mrs. Miles, Mrs. Miles. But there was no answering frisson, no clue at all.

Again, that sick panic climbed in her, and in an effort to control it, she got up. Physical action would help, she thought absurdly. Keep yourself moving, girl—

Beyond the dining room she could see a pair of doors, glass doors framing greenery and the wrought iron tracing of a glazed room beyond. To get back to her room she'd have to pass the big man, now drinking coffee and again staring consideringly at her. And she couldn't do that. She didn't know why, but she couldn't walk within touching distance of that big sombre figure.

Moving as smoothly as she could, she went towards the glass doors, and slipped through them, closing them behind her softly, almost as though any noise she might make would bring that frightening watcher after her.

The conservatory, for that it clearly was, smelled damp and hot and earthy, and she slid gratefully onto a wooden bench that was almost buried under the exuberant growth of trailing ivy that hung from the roof above it. There's probably spiders, the voice in her mind warned. I don't care if there are, she told the voice, returning to the silent conversation with herself she had been conducting all morning. I don't care if there are.

'Have you done your floor, then?' The voice sounded so close she jumped, and then shrank back amongst the trailing green, not wanting at this moment to see anybody.

'No – I'm not going to, neither, not till gone eleven. Finish early and that creep'll only find you something else to do. I've had some, I tell you. I'm not on piece work, I told him last time, and you can do what you like about it. Still, it saves a row if I don't get finished too early—'

Gingerly, Abigail peered through the greenery to the far side of the conservatory, but all she could see was a flash of white, there was so much vegetation filling the available space. A smell of cigarette tobacco filled the air gently, and she relaxed. Hotel staff, that was all, sneaking an illicit cigarette. Just like nurses—

'You very busy, then?' the first voice said.

'No – only got four. But I'll tell you what—' the voice dropped a little 'One of 'em's right off, I think.'

'Off? Nutty, you mean?'

'No – listen —' and the voice dropped again, so low that Abigail could only hear snatches of what was said. Not that she wanted to, anyway. Right now, all she wanted to do was sit here, in peace, and *think*, to continue on her private clue-hunt.

'Go on,' the first voice said, suddenly louder. 'You're just making it up. I don't believe a word of it. You're always imagining things like that. Like that feller last year you said was having it off with—'

'This *isn't* like that,' the other voice insisted. 'I tell you, I had a real close look at her, when I took in her tea. And it *is* her – it's just like the picture – here, you look for yourself.'

There was a rustle of newspaper, and then, suddenly the door from the dining room opened, and the manager came hurrying through.

Abigail took one frightened look at him, and got up, but he didn't see her, walking rapidly to the far corner of the conservatory. She moved quickly then, her heart suddenly beating hard, her mind spinning. That woman with the newspaper had been the chambermaid, the one who had brought her tea—

The manager's voice was raised suddenly, shouting at the maids, and grateful for the cover the noise afforded, Abigail slipped back through the double doors into the dining room. The big man had gone; there were only a couple of waiters lazily clearing tables. She hurried across the room, out into the lobby, and out through the open door, not knowing where she was heading.

It wasn't the front door as she had imagined, but led to a cobbled terrace that opened on to a wide quiet garden. And along the terrace were chairs and a table, a wrought iron table, with a row of newspapers on it. One of them, one of those papers carries a clue, Abigail heard her secret voice shout at her. Go through *all* of them, at once. One of them will be the one those women were looking at, and it has a picture in it. A picture of – who?

CHAPTER TWO

She went through the papers with a cold deliberation that almost surprised her. One after the other, business page, home news, cartoons, gossip diary, fashion, classifieds, sport, folding each one neatly when she had finished. It was one of the last, a tabloid, that carried it, tucked between a picture of a toothily grinning girl in a swimsuit so tight that her breasts bubbled over the top, and the announcement of a brand new contest. Win Your Dream Home, worth £5000. Enter Today—

There looking blandly up at her, the lines a little blurred, with trees and oblivious passers-by in the background, was her own face, the same narrow grave face with the long uptilted eyes that had looked back at her from her mirror so short a time ago.

I wonder where it was taken? she thought absurdly, and peered at the anonymous background behind the slight figure that was hers, yet seemed so strange. Looks like a park – Regent's Park, maybe. When did I have a photograph taken there? I can't remember—

She swallowed then, dryly, and forced herself to read the words beneath the picture. The print was big and bold, shouting blackly 'DO YOU KNOW THIS WOMAN?' and then running on in more subdued print, but with a breathless quality in the words.

'This is a woman the police very much want to talk to, needing her help in seeking nine year old Daniel Tenterden, the quiet dark-haired schoolboy who disappeared from home leaving behind only an ominously blood stained marble candlestick. Is she seeking him too, or does she know what has happened to him? If she sees this, or if anyone else recognizes her, the police want to talk to her —'

The panic rose again, higher and higher, so that the edges of her vision blackened and swirled sickeningly.

I won't faint, I won't – it isn't going to happen – but even as she began to let the words collect in her mind, she was moving, running headlong across the cropped grass of the lawn, towards its demure rim of trees and bushes. Ignoring the way branches snatched at her sweater and hair, she burst through the shrubbery and beyond, until the trees thickened, closed behind her, and delivered her headlong rush into a small grassy clearing. And there she let her knees fold, let herself crouch against the rough bark of a tree, to shake helplessly, staring unseeingly into the undergrowth that wrapped the little open patch in seclusion.

I don't believe it. I don't believe it. It can't be me. Some other woman, not me. I just look like her, that's all, it can't be me —

But it was, the hateful inner voice said. That was a picture of you. Even a maid who'd only seen you once spotted it. It was you.

But what does it all mean? Abigail thought piteously. Is this child dead? And if he is, did I have anything to do with it? Is that the emotional trauma that brought on this horrible terrifying not-knowingness, that sliced a year out of your consciousness? And this husband? What about him? Can so – so violent an experience as marriage be sponged out of memory just like that? Stepmotherhood – can that too disappear so completely? What went wrong with the marriage anyway, if it did happen? Why was he abroad after – well, it can't be even a year of marriage. Still the honeymoon —

'Oh, God,' she moaned softly. 'Please, help me remember. Please, *make* me remember. Give it all back to me, please. I can cope with anything if I understand, but not when I don't know. Please—' And she closed her eyes tightly, willing memory to come back.

Only blackness, with faint sparkles of light in it, spinning burrs of light that enlarged and then shrank to infinity, and started to spin again, bigger and bigger. Inside her closed lids she fixed her gaze on one of the spinning burrs, and it ran away into the blackness, enlarged, reddened —

She saw then, saw as though on an incredibly remote cinema screen, a room, big – yes big, for the corners were dark and shadowed, and there was heavy dark furniture. The screen widened, and the picture came closer. A low table. A lamp, with a red fringed shade on it – she could see that with intense clarity, the way a piece of the fringe was rucked up – a pool of light spilling over onto the floor. And in the pool of light, a small figure, lying still. Dark curly hair, with a patch where the curls shone stickily in the glow from the light, and her own hand coming out, her own hand with the scar on the knuckle of the forefinger, the scar left by that stupid parrot on children's medical who'd pecked her. Her hand, turning the child's head, moving him, so that the face came into the picture, blank, battered, the eyes turned up so that a rim of bluish white showed under the dark lashes – and then the burr of light, spinning into infinity, enlarging again. Only the dark redness of her closed lids to look at.

Slowly, feeling as shaken and weak as though she had just run a mile, she let her eyes open, let the daylight come through her lashes, let her eyes stare unseeingly into the greenness – and then sharply, she focused, and felt sick terror wash over her.

Leaning against a tree on the other side of the tiny clearing was the big dark man from the hotel. She stared at him, dumbly, unable to move or think, and he looked

22

back at her, not moving, but with the same unblinking stare that had so perturbed her at breakfast. And then he smiled, lifting the corners of his lips.

'Don't look like that.' His voice was very deep, but there was a clarity in the crisp way he bit off his words. 'I won't eat you.'

She tried to stretch her stiff lips into the semblance of an answering smile, thinking confusedly – I've got to put on a show – mustn't let anyone see there's anything wrong – and she had almost succeeded when he added, in a conversational tone 'And I won't give you away, either, Mrs. Tenterden.'

'No!' she almost shouted the word. 'I'm not – I'm —' she swallowed hard. 'I'm Abigail Lansdon. That is, at the hotel they called me —'

'Mrs. Miles,' he said softly. 'I know. Why is that, do you suppose?'

'I don't know,' Abigail couldn't keep back the awareness of her own helplessness, couldn't stop her voice sounding pitiful. And as she spoke, the tears started, welling from her eyes, blurring her vision, making her body shake.

The big man said nothing, standing there quietly against the tree, just watching her. And oddly, his very impassivity helped, made the tears stop coming, so that she stopped weeping, and took a deep shuddering breath.

'I think I know why,' he said then, as she looked up sharply.

'What?'

'Why you signed the register as Mrs. Miles last night, when you arrived here.'

'I—' she shook her head, trying to clear it. 'I did what?'

'Signed the register as Mrs. Miles,' he said with a heavy sort of patience that sent a twinge of irritation through her.

'Did I?'

'Come, my dear young lady! Surely you recall what you wrote in the register!' The scorn was back in his face, the same scorn that had so angered her earlier. And she leaned forwards, her hands flat on the ground on each side of her, and shouted at him, letting all the frustration and fear of the past couple of hours boil over into the luxury of fury.

'No I don't! I don't remember a bloody thing, not one thing! I'm running around in some crazy nightmare and I can't make any sense out of any of it, and I wish I were *dead*, do you hear me? And why don't you stop staring at me as though I were a moth in a bottle, and go to hell, whoever you are—'

'In due course, I have no doubt I shall,' he said equably. 'Have you quite finished that tirade? Has it made you feel better?'

Feeling suddenly foolish, she leaned back, dusting her hands free of grass and earth in what she knew was a childish gauche gesture. And nodded sulkily. 'Good,' he said. 'As I see it, you are in need of some assistance – friendship, perhaps we could call it? And since there is no one else about who seems willing to volunteer for the job – except of course the manager, whom perhaps you prefer?—'

She made a grimace, and he smiled faintly. 'Very well. You will have to settle for me. And since I appear to have some information about you that you lack, and need, I have no doubt you will see the wisdom of accepting my offer.'

It was strange how very much calmer she felt, how much more in command not only of herself but her situation. She settled herself more comfortably against the reassuring strength of the tree, and stared up at him, curiously. So calm, and so quietly insulting – yet with something about him that made her feel that perhaps he could be trusted, could help her find a way out of the maze.

'Who are you?' she asked abruptly.

He moved for the first time, sketching a mockingly ironic bow.

'My name is Max Cantrell, Mrs. Miles.'

Abigail flushed. 'Don't call me that! It isn't my name.'

'It's as much your's as Tenterden. Your husband's first name is Miles, so you are usually known as Mrs. Miles Tenterden. You simply dropped the surname when you arrived here last night.'

Anger began to stir again. 'How in hell do you know so much about me? And how do I know you're right?'

'It's my job to know facts. I'm a journalist.'

'I see! This begins to make some sense. Friendship, you offered? Of course – in exchange for which you fill your paper with all the juiciest garbage you can dig out. That sort of friendship you can keep—'

She got to her feet, shaking dead leaves from her skirt.

'I am not entirely without self interest, I admit,' Max said, unperturbed. 'But what choice have you? Who else will help you if I don't? The manager? I can imagine how much help *he'd be*. Other guests here? The chamber-maids?'

She began to move towards the edge of the clearing and the broken gap in the shrubbery through which she had burst.

'I'll go to – to – the police,' and indeed there didn't seem anything else she could do. The idea was so obvious – why hadn't she thought of it earlier?

'Oh certainly!' Max still hadn't moved. 'And get locked up for your pains. And then what hope of finding what happened to Daniel?'

'Daniel?'

'Your stepson.'

25

It happened again, sickening in its horrible familiarity, yet so intense it was like nothing she had felt before. The rising tide of black panic, the scream of terror climbing needle sharp inside her head, the clamouring of that secret voice deep in her mind—

He was holding her, his hands clamped hard on her arms at the elbows, keeping her on her feet. She let her head droop forwards and tried to breathe deeply, tried to keep control of herself until the panic receded, drawing some strength from the impersonal grip that almost hurt.

'Stop being a ninny,' he said, his voice gentler now. 'Getting into a state of dumb idiocy won't help in the slightest. You've got some sense. Use it.'

'I'm all right now. I'm sorry. It – it keeps happening.'

'There is no need to apologize,' he said. 'Just try not to give way to it again. You are all right now.' It was a statement, not a question.

'Yes.'

'Good. You'd better sit down again.'

Obediently, she sat beside the tree, curling her legs beneath her, and rested her head on the trunk. Max returned to his tree, to stand leaning against it in the same relaxed yet wary way.

'You can't remember anything about why you are here, how you got here?'

She shook her head, almost ashamed to admit her inadequacy.

'Then I'd better tell you all I know. I've been working on this story since it started, so there's quite a lot. Your husband, first.'

'It sounds so *odd*. To have a husband, I mean. Unbelievable.'

'You can believe it. It is perfectly true. I've seen the records at Somerset House.'

26

'I see.'

'It will help if you don't interrupt. Just listen,' and again, he produced that considering unsettling stare, so that she dropped her gaze for a moment. But then she sat up more erectly, and said quietly, 'Go on.'

'Miles Tenterden is a painter. A bad tempered morose type from all accounts. He used to live in France, in a tatty villa in Normandy – lived there for eight years, in fact. He went there when his first wife died, when his son was less than a year old.'

Max looked very grim suddenly. 'He was, it appears, so distressed by the death of this first wife that he couldn't cope with any of his responsibilities. He turned the child over to his wife's sister for care. There were no money problems – the child had inherited a great deal from his mother. And that was that. Until he suddenly remembered the boy needed an education. He came back to England to make arrangements to send him to boarding school, and managed to get himself injured in a road accident. He'd lived buried in the country so long he'd probably become careless of traffic. Anyway, he was admitted to hospital, and this is where you come into the picture.'

'Private Wing,' Abigail said suddenly.

'What?'

'I was working in the Private Wing – yesterday, I thought,' she smiled bleakly at him. 'It was yesterday when I went to bed, but a year ago when I woke up again this morning.'

'Yes. Well, Miles met you. And four weeks later married you.'

She stared at him in blank disbelief. 'Four *weeks*?'

Max nodded. 'Four weeks. Special licence, quiet wedding, the whole romantic bit.'

'I wish I could *remember*.'

He laughed then. 'I suppose that must be frustrating. To be the centre of a real life glamorous romance, and not even remember it!'

'That's – cruel,' she said quickly. 'I don't just want to remember for—'

He looked at her closely for a moment, and then made a small grimace. 'I'm sorry. I suppose I'm not really quite – well, never mind.'

'You're not quite sure you believe me, is that it? Not sure I really can't remember anything?' Abigail said levelly.

There was a pause, and then he smiled, a real smile, so wide and friendly that it lifted his face from its heavy cragginess into a much younger friendlier shape. 'Not now. I did doubt it, but not now. Your face is the expressive kind. You can't help showing what you're thinking. I believe you.'

'Thank you,' she said, and took a deep breath. Perhaps, after all, this man, story seeking journalist though he was, could be a friend?

'I'll tell you the rest. Miles took you to his home – the house where his sister-in-law and son were living, and you settled down, as they say. From here on in, I can only offer surmise – police surmise. As they see it, Daniel's stepmother – you – got jealous of the boy. And decided to get rid of him and enjoy, through his father, the money he'd inherited. The chance came when Tenterden, about ten months after his marriage, returned to Normandy to clear up his affairs there, collect his canvases and so on, before settling permanently in England again.'

He stopped, and then said abruptly 'The police suspect that the boy was in fact disposed of, and with such skill that no trace of the body can be found, only the mess left in the house giving any indication of what happened.

The puzzle now is not only the whereabouts of the boy, dead or alive, but also – you.'

The warmth of a few minutes earlier had quite gone from his face and his voice. He looked grim, his lips set in a heavy line as he stared at her.

'You think I did it,' she said helplessly. 'That I – killed the child. That's why you look like that.'

He frowned then, and shook his head. 'No. I am not convinced you killed your stepson. If I look – sour—it's because Tenterden makes me *sick*.' There was real anger in his voice. 'The man's a bastard. To abandon his child for so long and for his own selfish reasons, to behave so—'

It was curious, the wave of loyalty to the husband she didn't know, wouldn't be able to recognize if he arrived in the clearing at this moment. 'Perhaps the boy reminded him too much of his dead wife. If he'd cared a great deal for her, it's understandable.'

'Your husband he may be, but that's nonsense. The man's not worth a light, a selfish louse.'

Wearily, Abigail said 'Oh, God, I don't know. Maybe he is. I'm in no position to argue with you. I can't remember anything about any of it. It's all so crazy, really it is. I'm not the sort to get hysterical amnesia, but *I can't remember—*'

'Hysterical amnesia?'

'That's one kind. Then there's retrograde – after a head injury. It affects memory of what happened during and since the injury, and sometimes, quite a long period before it.'

'Couldn't yours be that kind?'

She looked startled. 'I suppose so. I'd rather assumed that it was hysterical—'

'How nice to find a woman who thinks of the least attractive thing first,' and he smiled his transforming smile again, 'Have you got any bumps anywhere?'

29

Gingerly, she felt her head. 'I don't think so—'

He came over, and pushing her head forwards, began to inspect her scalp. She giggled.

'You're just like the nurse we used to have at school. Nitty Norah, we called her—'

He ignored this. 'There does appear to be a bump here. I suppose you can't remember – no. Of course not.'

Wonderingly, Abigail explored the scalp above the nape of her neck, just where her skull curved down to meet it. The tender ridge there, that had escaped her hairbrush, didn't feel big enough to have caused so incredible a response as a retrograde amnesia stretching back to a year.

'It hurts a bit – so it must be recent—' she said.

'Excellent,' he said.

'Thank you!' Abigail said tartily. 'It's my head we're discussing, not yours—'

'Stupid woman,' Max said, but in an abstracted way that robbed the words of any sting. 'Excellent because it means you were hit by someone. It means you are less likely to have murdered this boy – that probably the person who hurt him hurt you too.'

She shook her head. 'It may convince *you* of my innocence – but will it convince anyone else? There's only my word that it hurts, this bump, anyway. So where do I go from here?'

'Do you accept my help?' Max asked.

She looked at him for a long moment, and then nodded. 'I've no choice,' she said simply.

'True' and he grinned at her. 'Right. This is what we do.'

CHAPTER THREE

He sat on the grass beside her, his arms round his knees. 'We start off by accepting as an undoubted fact your loss of memory.'

'Thank you,' she murmured, a little sardonically.

He didn't even have the grace to look embarrassed. 'It says a lot both for you, and for my power to suspend disbelief, that I do accept. It's a pretty novelettish concept, after all.'

'People read novelettes because they're believable, I suppose. So why say this is so difficult to believe?' She felt argumentative, as though she had to defend her own lapses before this grim man.

'Do you always go off at tangents like this?' he sounded genuinely curious. 'Can't you stick to the point ever?'

She grinned, a little wickedly. 'Perhaps, I can't remember—'

'All *right*. We accept you have a genuine amnesia, dating from the time you woke up this morning. But last night, when you checked in here, you *could* remember what had happened—'

'How can you know that?'

'Because you used your husband's first name as a pseudonym, and called yourself Mrs.—'

'Fair enough. I'm sorry I interrupted.'

'Try not to do it again. As I was saying, you knew what was what last night. So you must have had a reason for coming here from London.'

She creased her forehead, thinking hard. 'That makes some sense. From London – look, *where* is this place,

31

anyway? I don't know, you see, whatever I might have known last night.'

'Cirencester. Gloucestershire.' He turned and looked very closely at her, but she looked blankly back at him. 'Does that mean anything to you?'

She shook her head. 'I – I seem to have heard of it,' she said slowly. 'There was a girl I trained with who came from Gloucestershire – I think she mentioned the town once. Old Roman site, or something—'

'But it doesn't mean anything else to you?'

'No. Should it?'

'That's what I'm trying to find out,' he said with a return of his heavy patience. 'You must have had a reason of some kind. Obviously.'

'Obviously,' she echoed. And could think of nothing else to say.

There was a long pause, and then he went on. 'It's reasonable to assume your arrival here had something to do with the boy Daniel. Perhaps he's here, too, some-where—'

She stared at him, sudden hope stirring in her. 'Do you mean you think it's possible that – he isn't dead?'

'I'm hoping he isn't,' Max said sombrely. 'Certainly the police evidence suggests he – or someone – was injured, but in the absence of stronger evidence it's as reasonable to assume he's alive as that he's dead.'

She caught her breath then, and said in a low voice 'He *was* injured—'

'What?' He whirled then, and his voice hardened. 'What did you say?'

'Don't look at me like that!' she let her fear of him show in her voice, for indeed he now looked so angry that all her original distrust of him came bubbling back. 'I can explain—'

And as she did, the anger in his face settled down. 'This scrap of memory – is it a common thing to happen in people with amnesia?'

'God, I don't know, for sure,' she said wearily. 'I didn't take specifically psychiatric training. But I believe that it can happen. Memory, when it comes back, doesn't come in a great rush, but sort of builds up from fragments. I got a brief fragment of that sort, I suppose—'

He nodded. 'I see. Then my idea is a practical one.'

'What idea?'

'We're going to go around in this district, take a good look at it. And see if something triggers off memory in you. Gives a reason for your being here.'

'That indeed makes sense,' she stood up suddenly, feeling again the need for physical action. 'At least it would be *doing* something—I can't stand much more of this sitting about talking to myself.'

'Is that what you've been doing?'

She laughed then. 'Haven't I just! Positively schizoid I've been, or is it paranoic? Anyway, I've been listening to myself tell me what to do till my head spins. It – isn't as funny as it sounds, really.'

'No. I don't imagine it is.'

He got up too, and began to move towards the edge of the shrubbery.

'Come on then. Have you got a coat or something at the hotel?'

'I don't know – there may be one. I didn't really look—' she stopped suddenly. 'Look, you say I shouldn't go to the police?'

'Not at this point. There wouldn't be much sense in it, would there? They think you – killed Daniel. I'm hoping he's still alive, and that you'll be able to find him. Go to the police, and they won't give you the chance to look. *They* might not be able to believe so willingly in your amnesia.'

'Then I can't go back to the hotel.'

'Why not?'

She told him about the suspicious chambermaid and the picture in the newspaper. He listened carefully, and then nodded.

'I understand. Look, which room is yours?'

She concentrated for a moment. 'It's at the end of the corridor, last on the right.'

'I'll go back then, and see what's going on. If there's been no fuss, I'll pick up your coat and – have you a handbag?'

'Yes.'

'That too, then. If there *has* been a fuss, I'll bring all your gear, and you needn't ever go back. But cutting and running before there's any need to will create suspicion in the management. Hang on here. I won't be long.'

And he disappeared into the bushes, moving remarkably quietly despite his size, leaving Abigail a little bewildered, but with a curious sense of comfort. Rude he may be, but he did seem to believe her, to trust her, even though she might be a murderer. And his motive for helping her in the way he had offered was a reasonable one. Anyway, what choice had she?

He returned surprisingly quickly, carrying a brown suede coat over one arm, the brown bag dangling ludicrously from his big hand.

'All quiet,' he reported. 'I had a word with the chambermaid making my bed. It appears that the woman who looked after your room marched out in a rage a little while ago – something to do with being caught smoking—'

'And nothing was said about me being in the hotel?'

'Not a word. And believe me, if there was anything to

34

be told, that woman would have told me. She's an invete-
rate gossip. So there's nothing to worry about—'

He helped her into her coat – which fitted as well as
the other clothes, but was just as unfamiliar – and looked
at her thoughtfully.

'But we've got to be practical. The chambermaid
mayn't have said anything in the heat of job-losing – but
other people see the papers and may spot you. We'll have
to do something—'

She nodded. 'I think I know what will help – can we go
to a chemist's?'

'If you like – what for? Grease paint or something?'

'Very funny. Hair pins. Then I'll do a transformation
bit that should help.'

'All right. Come on then.'

They went quietly out of the shrubbery, and across
the deserted lawn, but Max swung to the left as they
reached the hotel and led her alongside the building,
past a noisy kitchen where pans clattered and voices were
raised in the hubbub of lunch preparation, to a small car
park. The car he unlocked was an elderly dark blue
estate one, rusty and shabby, but with none of the
clutter inside one expected to find in a car that is well
used.

He started the engine with a roar, and the car swung
out under a low archway, into a broad square shopping
street. There were cars parked in the centre of it, and on
the far side, a beautiful old church flung itself upwards in
sweeping flying buttresses and a lovely soaring tower that
hung delicately against the clear blue of the spring sky.

The place was quiet, yet gently bustling with shoppers
and children, and Abigail felt a moment of elation as she
took in the prettiness of the shop fronts past which they
drove. A pleasant town. I could be happy here – have
been happy here. The thought slid away, and she tried

to catch it, as Max swung left into another narrow shopping street, and stopped beside the curb.

'Hair pins, you say?'

'Mm? Oh, yes – look, I'll get them.'

'No you won't. The fewer people who see you before you've done your transformation bit, as you call it, the better.' He got out of the car, and left her with her head down, snuggled into the collar of her coat. It felt so odd, to be hiding from people's eyes like this—

When he came back, he thrust a small parcel into her hands and drove off, down the narrow street, left again into a quiet road lined with terraces of old houses.

'There's a mirror on the sun shade,' he said, and obediently, she pulled the shade down, and peered into the speckled mirror stuck on its reverse side. She found a comb in her handbag, and pulled the twist of hairpins he had bought out of their package. There were sunglasses in the package too, and she smiled as she saw them.

'Elementary, my dear Watson,' she murmured, and began to comb her hair back, pulling it with practised fingers into a neat french twist, pinning it firmly.

He looked at her approvingly. 'Good. It makes a considerable difference. Makes you look – younger.'

'It's supposed to make me look older. More severe,' she said a little petulantly. 'I wear it like this on duty.'

With the sunglasses, which were big and dark, she indeed looked quite different, but after peering at herself for another moment, she swept the fringe back from her forehead, and pinned that too, making a parting in the centre.

He nodded then, and said 'That'll do. Short of dyeing it black, you can't alter it much more. Right. Come on.'

And he started the car again, and drove away, taking them all round the town. It wasn't a very big town, and as they moved through the traffic, Abigail peered eagerly about her, trying with every fibre of her being to see something – anything – that was familiar, that would remind her of some episode in the past lost year. But there was nothing, not even a renewal of that moment of elation she had felt when she first saw the central square outside the hotel.

Four times he drove around the town, until every street had been traversed, every shop looked at. And still nothing. Neither of them spoke, but Abigail felt depression settle over them like a tangible thing.

'This isn't getting us far,' he said abruptly, pulling up outside a big grocer's shop in the main square. 'Lunch, I think, then we'll move out of the town for a while—'

'Lunch?' she said, alarmed. 'I'd have to take these glasses off in a restaurant – and even with my hair up, people might—'

'Wait here,' he commanded, and left the car quickly to disappear into the shop.

He was gone a long time, so long she began to fret, feeling as though the passers-by who looked casually at her were really recognizing her as that woman suspected of child murder, were hurrying straight to the police with their suspicions—

Nervously, she moved in her seat, turning her body so that she looked out across the broad roadway instead of at the pavement, keeping her head down. Between the parked cars that filled the centre of the road she could see glimpses of the opposite pavement, but reassured herself with the realization that it was too far away for any foot passenger there to recognize her. And then, she saw him.

A slight figure in a pale coat – a Burberry, perhaps. One of those military style raincoats, anyway. He wore the collar up, despite the bright sunshine, his sleek dark head poking forwards out of it in rather a tortoise-like fashion.

37

And then she realized he looked like that because he was staring fixedly through the traffic right at her.

She shivered suddenly, and slid even farther down in her seat. The sight of this stranger filled her with a cold fear, yet she felt her eyes pulled up almost against her will, until she was looking at the small figure again, there across the square. Why should he frighten her so? Just a man in a raincoat, lounging against a shop window, after all. Why did he seem so menacing?

Because you know him, her secret voice whispered. He isn't a stranger. And her need to know overcame her fear, so that she leaned forwards, staring intently at him, trying to force her memory to release another fragment of the puzzle. Behind her, the car door clicked and opened and, startled, she turned her head. Max got in, and turned to put a couple of bulging paper sacks on the rear seat.

'Sorry to be so long. Sleepy shops in sleepy towns don't know how to hurry themselves – but I've got a reasonable collection for a picnic lunch—' His voice sharpened as he looked at her. 'What's the matter? Have you – remembered something? You look grim—'

'There's a man over there,' she said breathlessly. 'He – I don't know who he is, but he – frightens me. Who is he?'

'Where?'

She turned again, indicating the other side of the road with a jerk of her head. 'There – by that toyshop window—'

But there was no one there. All she could see now between the serried ranks of parked cars was the shop window, the red, blue and yellow of the toys displayed inside it, the gilt of the lettering on the facia above. But no sign of the man in the pale Burberry.

'He's gone—' she said stupidly.

'Who was he?' Max asked sharply.

She lost her temper then, and shouted at him. 'How

38

the hell do I know? I *told* you – he frightened me, but I don't know why. Asking me stupid questions is as much good as telling me to fly to the moon. Or are you trying to catch me out in some fashion? Still not convinced I can't remember? If that's all—'

'Shut up,' he said, and took her shoulders in his impersonal grasp and shook her so that her head snapped from side to side. 'We'll have a little less hysteria, and a little more of that common sense you can display when you try. Now. Tell me slowly and quietly. What did he look like? And have you any idea why he frightened you?'

She took a deep shuddering breath. 'I'm sorry. I shouldn't have lost my temper. But it's – difficult to be sensible when I'm feeling so frightened, so lost and—'

'I know. Forget it. Now, tell me.'

'He – wasn't very tall. Thinnish. And dark. He had that sort of polished look some men have. Smooth hair, you know?'

'Like the hotel manager?'

She concentrated for a moment, trying to put herself back at the head of the hotel staircase, looking down at the man at the desk. Yes, he'd had that sleek shiny patent-leather head, the narrow shoulders – her face cleared.

'I'm sorry,' she said again. 'I'm like a puppy on fireworks night, jumping at every creak in the woodwork. Of course that was it. That man over the road looked like the manager – maybe it *was* him. And he scared me this morning, nasty smarmy creature that he was—'

'Are you sure?'

'How do you mean?'

'You don't think perhaps it was someone from that lost year of yours? Someone involved in this business with Daniel?' He leaned towards her, and looked very closely at her. 'Try something – Abigail. Close your eyes—'

After a moment, she did, thinking absurdly – he called me by my name. Nice—

'—and concentrate. He's there again, and you're looking at him. By the shop window. Can you see him?'

She tried, there behind her closed lids, to see the man. She could see the Burberry, the cars on each side, even a woman pushing a pram coming momentarily between the man and the edge of the pavement, just as when she had actually been staring across at him. But the face – that was a blank. Just a figure with a tortoise-peering head but no features on it. Yet a feeling of cold fear wrapping round her at the sight of him—

She must have been shaking, because Max's arm was across her shoulders, and he was saying 'All right – take it easy. Give up trying, and let it come when it's ready – and maybe it was the manager, anyway. Forget it, and we'll go and have some lunch. You need some.'

She leaned back in her seat as he started the car and pulled away from the curb, staring blindly out of the window as they drove out of the town, and along gradually narrowing roads into the quiet of the countryside. By the time he stopped driving again, she felt better, only the memory of her fear leaving a faint lingering flavour in her mind.

Max got out of the car, and lugged out the paper sacks of food. 'Come on,' he said briefly. 'This looks remote enough. And I'm hungry, too.'

CHAPTER FOUR

There was a game paté and a fresh cool cucumber, slices of locally cured ham and richly pink tongue, potato crisps, and juicy tomatoes, and a crusty french loaf, still warm from the baker's oven. He'd bought a piece of ripe Brie cheese, too, and crisp green apples and a few early cherries. She ate greedily, for she hadn't realized how hungry she was. And when he produced a bottle of wine, an unusual sparkling burgundy with the body of a red wine but the refreshing tingle of a light rosé, the picnic became almost a celebration.

And the place he'd found for their lunch enhanced the meal. They sat on sheep-cropped grass, with a tiny wooded copse behind them, and a small hill falling away at their feet into a chequer board of neat fields, some showing the tender green of early crops, others with the rich brown of newly turned ploughed furrows over which birds swooped and fought for exposed worms. There were bluebells in the cool wood behind them and the light breeze brought the delicate scent of them over their heads. And there were sounds, too, country sounds, of birds, and distant farm machinery chugging, and far away a train moving across the pretty landscape. It all added up to peace and contentment, making the darkness of Abigail's fears, the mystery that this morning had seemed so terrifying, somehow irrelevant.

She lay back contentedly, dropping her empty paper wine cup beside her, and stretched hugely.

'I could sleep for a week,' she said drowsily. 'Sleep and sleep and wake up a year ago with none of this having happened.'

'I thought you'd enjoyed this lunch.'

'Oh, I'm sorry! I didn't mean that—' she sat up and looked at him, and smiled apologetically. 'Of course I did. You've been – marvellous, really. And I am grateful for your help—'

'All in a day's work,' he said, sounding suddenly chilly.

'Of course.' The return to his usual sardonic manner sparked her anger again. 'I mustn't waste your time. You've got a story to write, haven't you?'

'Eventually. When there's something to write about. So we'd better get on our way.'

Immediately she stood up, the magic of the early afternoon peace and sunshine quite gone. In silence they packed up the remains of their picnic, which he buried tidily under piles of rotting leaves in the copse, and went back to the car. And in silence they started their peregrinations again, moving from village to hamlet, along country lanes and major roads, while Abigail sat erect and tense beside him, staring out at the passing scenery, willing herself to remember – anything at all, but *remember*.

The afternoon stretched itself, lengthening the shadows, as cottages and houses, blank fields and walled gardens, woods and little bridged streams disappeared behind their swishing wheels. The roads filled with cars full of mothers and children coming home from school, and emptied again, and still they moved over the landscape, quartering square mile after square mile. And nothing she saw held any promise of memory, no triggers clicked in her mind, no clues at all came out of what she stared at so fixedly.

They spoke hardly at all. Sometimes at a cross roads, Max would say 'Left or right?' and she would just shrug and mutter 'I don't know – I'm sorry' and they would drive on.

The sky had washed itself clear of colour, turning a soft blueish grey before, by tacit consent, they made their way back to the town. She sat beside him miserably, lost on a new wave of sick anxiety. There seemed no answer anywhere in this impersonal Cotswold country, no possible reason for her being there. And the depression that filled her made her very bones ache with unhappiness.

When he stopped the car, in the car park of the hotel, she stirred herself, and said heavily 'It's no use, is it? I might as well go to the police now, and be done with it. I'm wasting your time.'

'You give up very easily. We've only covered one side of the area so far – the East. Tomorrow we'll start on the other side. No need to get so low yet.'

'If you're so sanguine about the outcome, why have you been so silent and bad tempered all afternoon?' She let her misery spill over into irritation. 'You're obviously regretting ever getting involved with me—'

He raised his eyebrows at her, and even in the dim light she could see the familiar scorn on his face. 'Have I said I have any regrets? If I was quiet it was because we were doing a job. If I'd filled the afternoon with scintillating chatter, you wouldn't have been able to concentrate at all. Are you the sort of woman who thinks every minute has to be filled with pointless gossip?'

'No, I'm not!' she flashed at him. 'But I'm – I'm lost and frightened and a little human warmth would go a long way towards helping. Or are *you* the sort of man who doesn't know what it is to be warm and friendly?'

He was quiet for a second, and then spoke in the friendlier voice he sometimes used. 'No. I've as much awareness as you of the value of friendship, believe me. But I don't want to – complicate things. I've said I'm going to help you sort out this whole lousy problem, and I will. Then, and not before, there'll be time for – friendship. In the meantime, let me assure you – when I'm quiet, it doesn't mean I'm bad tempered, or anything other than abstracted. Can you accept that?'

'Oh – I suppose so. My God, but you've got a marvellous trick of putting me at a disadvantage, haven't you? You make me feel a complete idiot. And whatever I may have forgotten, one thing I do know -- I'm *not* an idiot!'

He laughed then. 'No, you're not. And you're standing up to a very nasty situation with a great deal of courage. It's my turn to apologize. Look, I'll make a deal with you. We'll forget all about the whole thing for a few hours, shall we? We'll go and get ourselves some dinner somewhere, and behave like ordinary civilized people out for an evening's entertainment. What do you say?' and he held out his hand.

She stared at him for a moment, peering at him in the deepening darkness, and then, suddenly tired, held out her own hand. 'All right. We'll do just that.' They shook hands solemnly.

He got out of the car and helped her out, pulling her coat over her shoulders against the chill of the evening air.

'I'll go in first. Give me a few minutes, and then follow me. If there's no hue and cry after you, you'll be able to go up to your room and freshen up. I'll meet you in the lobby in fifteen minutes or so—'

She watched him disappear into the lighted building, standing in the shadow of the car for fully five minutes before following him. The lobby was empty, and she slipped up the stairs to her room like a wraith. Even if there were no hue and cry, as Max had put it, she felt too drained and weary to want to meet anyone, least of all that unpleasant smarmy manager—

As she washed and changed, she thought again about the morning, about the man in the light coloured Burberry who had stared at her across the square, but already her memory was blurred. Had that man been the manager, or someone else? And if someone else – who? Why had he seemed so familiar to her?

Irritably, she shook herself. 'We'll forget about the whole thing for a few hours—' Max had said. And it was good advice. However hard she tried, memory eluded her. Better to try to forget it all, because that way perhaps memory would be lulled, would allow itself to slip through the defences of her amnesia and bring the answers with it. So, she put on the white blouse and the black suit, amused to see how very elegantly they suited her, and brushed her hair out before pinning it up again in its rather severe french twist. No need to court trouble by looking too much like that newspaper photograph.

There were friendly sounds coming from somewhere as she let herself out of her room, but the corridor was deserted. She stood poised for a moment, and then, moving softly in her high heeled black shoes, the ones she had found tucked into a pocket of the suitcase, she went to the head of the stairs and looked down into the lobby. She was half way down the stairs before she noticed them standing just outside the door onto the terrace, and stopped frozen with sudden fear.

There were two of them, and when she recognized Max's burly shape she relaxed momentarily – until she heard his voice, slightly raised in answer to the low murmur of something the other man had said – a tall man she had never seen before.

'Look, inspector, I can explain a good deal. It's not particularly—'

She heard no more in the wave of sheer panic that overcame her. Inspector! A policeman, a policeman looking for her, for the woman of the photograph – and Max had said she mustn't go to the police for fear of being

45

disbelieved. Yet here he was *talking* to the police. Handing her over—

She was so frightened that for a moment she swayed on the edge of a faint, but somehow she managed to keep hold of herself, managed to move silently backwards until she was in the upstairs corridor again, staring round wildly, wanting only one thing – an escape route. Behind her, from the lobby, she heard the men's voices again, heard them come in from the terrace, and in terror she ran along the corridor, back past her own room.

She was in luck. There was another staircase there at the far end, a narrow one, probably for the staff, and careless of being seen she fled down it as though all the hounds of hell were after her. At the foot there was a small lobby, cluttered with laundry baskets and crates of empty bottles, and beyond them, a door. She seized the handle, and for one sick moment thought it was fastened, that she was trapped, but the key was in the lock, and she turned it with cold shaking fingers, to almost fall through.

She was in the car park again, near the noisy kitchens, and desperately she ran past them, not caring for the clatter she made as she kicked an empty oilcan by the door, running headlong – anywhere to escape from the men she was quite sure were behind her.

She came out under the little archway, and without thinking lurched sideways to go along the pavement. It wasn't until she was abreast of the brightly lit entrance that she realized she was passing the main door of the hotel, realized that there on the steps was the Inspector – and wheeled and ran again, across the square, dodging through the few cars that still were parked in the centre of it.

Behind her she heard a shout, and ran harder, not caring where she ran to. There were iron gates in front of her suddenly, open gates, and she ran between them into shadows under trees, running for the shelter of the big building that loomed before her.

It was the church, she realized as she felt rough stones against her outstretched hands, felt herself checked by the weight of the building before her, and she stopped, almost sobbing with breathlessness, leaning her hot cheek against the roughness of a buttress, gulping the cool night air into her painfully tearing lungs.

After a moment, she lifted her head, and tried to listen, putting all her concentration into her straining ears. Above the thumping of her own pulses she could hear cars, and above them the sounds of footsteps, moving along the pavements of the square, but no more shouts. But were some of the footsteps coming nearer? She couldn't be sure and although she was still gulping for breath she started to move, pulling herself along the wall, seeking darkness and a hiding place.

The wall turned, and she saw that she had reached a corner, and that beyond it, the church was floodlit. No escape that way. She turned then, and began to move back towards the comforting dimness of the churchyard – and then she heard it. There *were* footsteps, heavy ones, very close, moving alongside the wall she was clinging to.

She whirled again and plunged forwards into the blackness of the churchyard, so very black in contrast to the floodlighting behind her. But in that darkness there was a hiding place, somewhere. There had to be.

Tussocks of grass clutched at her feet, and big gravestones loomed up to hit cruelly at her shins, tearing her skin into painful grazes, but she ignored them, for now the footsteps could be heard again, not crunching on the gravel of the pathway beside the church wall, but thudding on the turf of the graveyard – running footsteps now, coming closer.

47

She ran faster, ignoring the hazards of humped graves and leaning moss-covered stones, until suddenly she found herself at a railing, and turned, almost weeping with fear, to scramble alongside it, seeking for a way out like a hunted animal that hears the hounds baying at its heels.

And then there was a small gate, swinging on rusty hinges, and she pushed on it, almost screaming with terror when the old metal shrieked protestingly, but she was through, into a badly lit side street. Now she could run in good earnest, and she fled up the centre of the little road, past shuttered shabby shops, over greasy hard cobbles, from one pool of light thrown from each weak street lamp to the next. And the running footsteps came after her, coming closer—

It was as though she had been running all her life, as though she would go on running until she fell dead of exhaustion onto slippery grass beneath her feet. For the road had come to an end and there were no more street lights. She was in an open space, a small hilly place, with only dim starlight to guide her, and those thudding footsteps coming closer and closer, until they were right behind her, and a heavy shape came up and loomed over her, until she could hear another person breathing heavily, above the tearing gasps that were ripping her own body into strings of pain.

And her terror made her try to push her failing body that little bit harder, made her try to pump her trembling legs into another spurt of speed – and failed. She was falling, her right foot clutched agonizingly, twisting her ankle as she felt her body swoop forwards. But before she hit the ground, even as she flinched from the blow she knew was coming from the earth beneath her, she was caught, was pulled up and away from herself, felt herself poised in mid air, and then held against a warm body in a hard strong grasp.

She had lost her freedom, had not found the oblivion of a hiding place, and she felt hot tears fall down her face as she struggled helplessly against the grip that held her so firmly, heard her own voice saying 'No–no–no–' with a sick husky repetition that sounded as though it were coming from farther and farther away—

Someone was crying, with thick tearing sobs, crying piteously. Poor thing, thought Abigail. Poor poor thing. It hurts her so to cry like that. Hurts her chest and her throat and ankle, why doesn't she stop crying like that, poor thing? And then she saw the dark sky above her, with its powdering of stars, and realized, almost with surprise, that it was her own chest and throat and ankle that hurt so dreadfully, her own sobbing she was listening to.

Gradually, the crying stopped, gradually the pain in her chest and throat subsided, although her ankle still throbbed sickenly, and then she was lying, almost comfortably, staring up at the sky above her and wondering disjointedly why she was lying there at all, and what had happened, and from where the warmth that comforted her aching back was coming.

'All right now?' The voice came from behind her, and startled, she turned her head and looked up, and discovered that she was lying with her head against Max's chest, with his arms holding her, and that it was the warmth of his body that she could feel.

'What?' she said stupidly, her voice thick and husky.

'Are you all right now? Have you hurt yourself anywhere?'

'I don't – what happened? Where—' and then she remembered, and struggled to sit upright, to pull away from him.

'Where is he? That Inspector – he was running after

49

me. Where is he? I've got to get away – he was trying to catch me—'

He pulled her down again, almost roughly. 'You young idiot. There's no Inspector chasing you—'

'I heard him – you—' And then she remembered the way Max had talked to the man in the hotel, and her terror came back, and she began to struggle against his firm grasp. 'You – it was *you*. You were telling the police about me – telling them where I was—'

'No I wasn't!' he said roughly, and almost shook her. 'Don't be so bloody stupid. If I'd wanted to hand you over to the police I could have done so any time this past twelve hours. I told him you'd gone – told him I'd seen you at the railway station this afternoon – and he'd have believed me if you hadn't suddenly gone galloping past the hotel with your ears laid back like some bolting rabbit. Still and all, I managed to head him off. I imagine he's still belting around in the town somewhere. It was me who ran after you – trying to stop you before you ran head first into his arms.'

He lifted her then, so that she was held against him even more closely, with her head resting on his shoulder, and his grip was still firm, but warmer now, more comforting than frightening.

'You silly child,' his voice was little more than a whisper. 'Silly, silly child, running like that. You could have killed yourself, you were so panic stricken—'

The gentleness in his voice was so warming, so very much what she needed at that moment that she clung to him, burying her hot tear-streaked face in his neck, making her clutch at him, so that he began to rock her, as though she were a baby needing soothing. And after a moment she raised her head, and tried to look into the face that was so near, tried to explain how frightened she had been—

For an interminable moment they stared at each other in the darkness, and then almost against her will, she put up her hand to touch his face. Her fingers brushed his lips, and then his head came down, and they clung together in a kiss that made her body dissolve and reform into a desperate tearing need for him, made her tremble with an intensity of wanting so strong that all her pain and misery melted away as though it had never been.

CHAPTER FIVE

'Oh my God,' she said, and then, absurdly, giggled.

There was a pause, and then Max said softly 'I didn't mean that to happen. I promise you I didn't mean that to happen. But you looked so – bereft, so miserable. I'm sorry.'

'It takes two,' she said, and put her hand up again to touch his cheek, and he turned his head and kissed her hand, sending another ripple of delight through her. 'Don't say you're sorry. I couldn't bear it if I thought you hadn't really wanted to.'

He laughed then. 'Oh, I wanted to. I've wanted to kiss you all day. That's why I was so surly this afternoon. Why I bit your head off every other time you said anything. It's easier to hide real feelings behind a display of bad temper. But I'm still sorry. Not for kissing you, but because this complicates things so—'

She pulled away from him, and looked up at him in the darkness, trying to see the expression of his face. And then made a little grimace herself.

'I – suppose it is. I'm – I mean, we're looking for my stepson, aren't we? I'm *married*—'

'Yes. You're married. And now you've remembered that, how does it make you feel?'

'But I haven't remembered it! I mean, I've remembered that you told me I'm married, but I can't remember the fact. I can't remember my – husband, or how I feel – felt – about him, or anything. All I know now is that it couldn't have been – I mean, couldn't *be* much of a marriage.'

'An involved speech, that. How can you be so sure it

isn't much of a marriage if you remember nothing about it?'

'Because you made me feel the way you did when you kissed me,' she said simply. 'If I'd been in love with someone else, even someone I couldn't remember, being kissed by you might have been pleasant, on a purely – well, physical level. But it couldn't have been what it was.'

'And just what was it?' and he whispered the words.

She swallowed. 'I can't explain properly. Special. Not just – a physical thing alone, but – well, *special*—'

And then his arms went round her again, and again they merged into one straining creature, again clung together so closely that it seemed they would never be able to separate. And when, breathless, she tried to pull away from him, he went on kissing her, her face, her eyes, the corners of her mouth and her neck, and she lay helplessly against him, caring nothing for yesterday or tomorrow, only letting herself be swept along in the heaven of now.

'Abigail. Abigail,' he was murmuring, saying her name as though it were a caress. 'Dearest Abigail. We'll sort this out, I promise you. It *will* be all right, I promise you that, and then nothing ever will spoil this for us, nothing at all. I promise. Abigail—'

His words pulled her down from her peak of joy then, and she pulled away from him, putting her hands flat against his chest and pushing so that he had to stop.

'Max – don't. No more. Please, Max—'

'Why? Isn't – isn't this special any more?'

'More special. That's why. We – we can't just be us, not yet. We've no right to. We're only making it worse for ourselves, going on like this. Aren't we? And anyway – the middle of the Humpy-Dumps is no place to make love—'

He stopped then, and in the darkness she felt rather

than saw him stiffen. Then he said softly, 'All right, my love. All right. So where do we go from here?'

She moved her injured leg tentatively, and very carefully got to her feet, Max helping her, so that she stood leaning against him, his arm round her. For a moment the sky swooped, and then regained its equilibrium, and she lifted her face and took a deep breath.

'Come on,' she said, and rested her head against his comforting chest. 'There's a way out to the road over there – where those trees are – can you see?'

Slowly they started to walk, pushing the rough grass away beneath their feet, and the pain in her ankle dwindled and became no more than a pleasantly exquisite pang each time she put her foot to the ground. She felt dreamlike, as though she were moving through a mad grey landscape in her mind, while her body lay wrapped in peace and comfort and happiness far away in a deep black bed. Even his voice sounded remote and dreamlike in her ears, even the voice that could make her body respond with the same pleasure that his touch did.

'Abigail—' he murmured. 'Abigail. You've remembered. Tell me what you've remembered. Where are we going?'

'There's a short cut across there,' she said, almost in a surprised way. 'Just across there. A short cut. You'll see—'

And even though she knew where the short cut was, even though she knew now that they were on the Humpy-Dumps, that undulating grassy stretch on the outskirts of the town, she couldn't have said how she knew, or where she was letting her feet take her. Just that she had to follow the short cut until they got there, there where the answer was waiting for them.

And when they reached the uneven road, still she knew where her dream wanted her to go, and turned to the right, hobbling along the rough tarmac between low grey hedges, with Max, big comforting Max holding her up safely and peacefully and wrapping her in a love she felt she had been waiting for her all her life.

The road turned, and narrowed, and she stopped, and Max, silent and attentive, stopped too.

'In there,' she whispered. 'In there.'

And stared into the darkness at the shape she knew so well. A cottage, the grey of its stone only marginally lighter than the grey of the night sky. Forsythia, pale grey now, but flaming yellow in daylight, growing beside the broken gate. A green painted gate, she knew, though here in the night it was just another shade of monochrome. Trees, whispering droopingly elegant laburnums, and stumpy cheerful apple trees, and a Japanese cherry that exploded in April into puff balls of sterile pink blossom.

'The blossom fell early this year,' she whispered. 'So early. It was all gone when we got here—'

She felt Max rigid beside here. 'When *we* got here?' and his own voice was a whisper, no louder than the gentle soughing of the night breeze through the laburnums.

'Yes – all fallen and brown and slippery on the path,' she said, and started to move forwards again. The gate swung awkwardly and creaked as she pushed on it, and somewhere, as though in answer, an owl called mournfully, and then repeated its cry a little farther away, seeming to flee from them as they moved up the stone flagged pathway towards the heavy door lost in the blackness of the wooden porch that hung over it so secretly.

'In there—' Abigail whispered again, and Max put out his hand, and pushed on the door. It opened, creaking just as the gate had, and again, as if on a pre-arranged cue the owl hooted, so far away now that the sound died and fell even as it reached them.

Beyond the door was an even deeper more velvety

blackness, and Abigail stood poised, still feeling like a remote observer of her own dream, still feeling her own body wrapped in the depths of sleep somewhere far away. Max moved beside her, fumbling in his pockets, and then there was a scratching sound, and a light sprang up, so bright and flickering that involuntarily she shaded her eyes against its brilliance.

He cupped the match in his hand, and held it high, peering beyond the small area it illuminated towards the interior of the cottage.

'In there—' Abigail said yet again, and moved forwards. Quickly, Max pulled her back, and went in first. As they stepped over the sill of the door, the match spluttered and went out, and Max caught his breath in pain as with its dying spurt it singed his fingers. He lit another, and round his shoulder, Abigail could see the room that the door led directly into, the table in the middle, the long horse hair settee with the shiny black cover and big buttons and the curly head rest, the dead kitchen range with a few cold ashes scattered in the hearth.

Max moved away from her, into the centre of the room. 'There's a candle here—' he said, and after a moment, the room filled with the soft yellow light of wax, and she saw he had lit a small stump of candle that had been jammed into an ancient brass candlestick. And she could see the rest of the room, the heavily rose-patterned old wallpaper, the deep window with rose patterned curtains, and a glass jam jar full of drooping dying bluebells on its broad sill; the rocking chair with its patchwork cushions; the dresser with its rows of willow patterned plates and saucers, and matching cups dangling mutely from a row of white hooks; the tea caddy with a picture of Windsor Castle on each of its six sides. But no living person apart from themselves.

'He's gone—' she said stupidly. 'He's gone—'

Max moved swiftly then, coming to face her and take her elbows in his familiar firm grip, putting his face close to her's:

'Who's gone, Abigail? *Tell* me. You've got to – who was supposed to be here?' And his voice was peremptory, not whispering any more.

And then the bubble burst, the dream she had been moving through so peacefully this past half hour or so, and she felt her head swim sickeningly, felt the pain in her ankle more vividly, and stared round in terrified bewilderment at the room. And put her hands up to her face and wept like a baby, all the weariness and terror and excitement she had gone through collapsing into sick anticlimax.

He almost carried her to the horsehair couch, stretching her aching trembling body on it and sitting beside her, stroked her face gently until her tears stopped, and she lay exhausted and shaking, staring up at him.

'What is this place, Abigail?' he asked gently. 'How much can you remember? Put it into words, my love – you'll find it easier to remember if you do—'

'I'm trying to—' she said piteously. 'Truly I'm trying to – just give me time – I'm trying to.'

He nodded, after a moment, and got up and began to prowl around the small room. Only the table had anything on it that seemed to show signs of recent human occupation. Apart from the stump of candle in the wax spattered candlestick there was half a bottle of milk, the cream on the top of it settled into a sourly wrinkled yellow layer, and a greaseproof wrapped package. Max picked it up, and a couple of curled sandwiches fell out. He turned the paper over, and was just about to put it back on the table when he stopped, and peered at it more closely. Then, he picked up the candlestick and came to sit on the settee again beside her.

57

'Look,' he said, and his voice sounded crisp and loud in the silence of the cottage. 'There's something written on this.'

She pulled herself up, and looked over his shoulder, trying to read the round unformed letters that sprawled across the grease stained paper. The candle leapt as her breath disturbed it, and settled again, and she could see the words more clearly.

'I've gone home to Auntie Cissie. She won't let him hurt me. If I stay here with you and he finds me, then he'll find you too and maybe he will hurt you as well and I wouldn't want that to happen. I can't look after you properly so I must go back. Auntie Cissie will think of something to help us. If she can't herself then she can always ask M who likes me I think though like I told you I like you better than both of them.

Love

Danny

And as she read the words, memory came surging back into Abigail, making her almost breathless as a few more pieces of the jigsaw clicked into place – and even as the memories swirled and settled, a sense of almost overpowering fear followed them, and made her clutch at Max's arm so that he winced.

'He mustn't go there,' she cried, her voice shrill and urgent. 'He mustn't – it's dangerous – we've got to get him back – he'll be—'

And now Max firmly lay her back against the cold surface of the settee, and said very crisply 'Abigail! Pull yourself together. Tell me exactly what you remember – right *now*. It's imperative you tell me, d'you hear? Right now—'

She turned her head fretfully from side to side. 'I can't remember a lot – just bits and pieces. Listen. There's a house. A big old house. It smells old. In London somewhere – I can't remember where, but it's in London. It's that name – Cissie – it makes me remember that house. Cissie – I can't remember who Cissie is, but it makes me remember that house, and I'm frightened – so frightened Max. Why am I so frightened? Who is Cissie?'

'Tenterden's sister-in-law,' Max said, and his voice brought her up sharply.

'Who? How do you know? How can—'

'The newspaper reports,' he said impatiently. 'Her name is Cecily – Cecily Brough. She's the one who looked after Daniel before his father married you—'

'Yes – yes, that's right. You told me – but Max – Max!' Fear began to rise in her again. 'Max, why am I so frightened of that house? I can feel it, all thick and horrible, the fear in the place—'

'That's what we've got to find out,' he said, soothingly. 'And we can. Listen to me, Abigail. Close your eyes.' She stared up at him, still feeling fear crawling in thick tendrils through her, but he said insistently 'Close your eyes.' And after a moment, she did. His voice sounded warm and strong, making the tendrils of fear curl up and away and hide themselves, waiting for another chance to come springing out at her.

'You are in the dark, Abigail, and there are pictures coming – like the one that came this morning. Let the pictures come, and describe them to me—'

Obediently, she stared at the swirling pinpoints of light in the darkness behind her eyes, let them get bigger and then diminish and grow again – and the pictures formed, tiny distant pictures that grew and became less wavering as she stared at them.

'I'm in a room,' she said, and her voice seemed distant, as though it belonged to someone else. 'A big room – a bedroom. Yes. A bedroom. There's a big mirror on the wall, and a smell of soap and perfume, and I can see

59

myself in the mirror, and it's not very light. Only the bed-side light is on. And—'

The picture wavered, lost its shape and was almost over-come by the swirling pinpoints of light. 'I can't see any-thing else—'

'Yes you can. Concentrate.' Max's insistent voice made the picture regain its definition. 'Just concentrate. The boy – is he there?

'No. He's downstairs. Downstairs. He ought to be in his bed and asleep, but he's downstairs and the woman is crying, sitting in the shadows and crying because Danny's downstairs and she's afraid. She says something bad is going to happen to him – Danny – I've got to go and get him – I must get him—'

And with the suddenness of a film, the picture she was staring at shimmered and disappeared, and another came to take its place. A low table. A lamp with a fringed red shade, and a piece of the fringe rucked up. A pool of light spilling over onto the floor. A small figure lying still. It was the same picture she had seen that morning – so long ago, that morning. And helplessly she watched it happen again, her own hand with its familiar scar coming down and turning the child's head, and the blank battered little face.

But this time it was different. As the picture faded and turned into burrs of spinning light, she felt an excruciat-ing pain at the back of her head, so strong that she whim-pered and moved, and opened her eyes, and saw Max's anxious face peering at her.

'Oh my God,' she whispered, staring at him with horror. 'My God, it was true—'

He put his arms round her and held her close. 'What was true, my darling? Tell me what was true.'

'I – Danny's father – my husband—' and saying the word made her suddenly sick. 'My husband. He was the

60

one who hurt Danny so badly. It must have been him. He must still have been there when I found Danny – still there, and he hit *me* – it was he who made me forget. Oh, Max – Max—' she began to weep again, great helpless tears falling down her face. 'Why did I marry him? How could I have married him, Max? How could I have let myself—'

'Perhaps you loved him,' Max said in a curiously flat voice.

She shook her head furiously. 'No – no! How could I have done? How could I possibly have loved him and still feel as I do about you? It just isn't—'

'How do you feel about me?' he stared at her very straightly, just as he had in the hotel that morning, but this time she wasn't frightened. She smiled up at him, a watery smile, but a smile all the same.

'I don't know. I haven't had time to sort it all out yet. But I feel – oh, *special*—'

And he laughed, throwing his head back and shouting his laughter, before holding her very close again and kissing her very thoroughly indeed. Abigail began to feel a lot better, suddenly. Safer, happier. Until she remembered again.

She pulled back from him, and said breathlessly, 'This is wicked. Wicked. Danny's in trouble somewhere. He's gone back to that house, and someone there – his father – someone's going to hurt him again. We've got to get him—'

Immediately he released her, and said soberly, 'Yes. Of course. Of course – but I wish you could remember how he came to be here.'

She shook her head, helplessly. 'I can't. Or even why I know this place at all—'

'Yet you knew where it was, you knew the name of that patch of open land we were on—'

'Yes. I did, didn't I?' Experimentally, she sat up. A new strength seemed to have come to her, and her head remained clear; even her ankle seemed less painful. 'Yet I'm certain I never knew the town up to a year ago – up to the time I can remember everything clearly, I mean—'

He helped her to her feet, but when she began to walk towards the door and winced when she put her injured foot to the ground, he stopped her.

'Look, you can't walk out of here, that's obvious. And if ever a girl needed a night's rest, it's you—'

'No!' she turned and clutched the lapels of his jacket. 'No, Max, we've *got* to go after Danny. *Now*. Go to London, and—'

She stopped and stared at him in consternation. 'Max – *where* in London? I don't know where the house *is*—' Her voice rose shrilly, a hint of hysteria coming into it.

Soothingly, he took her hands, gently disentangling her grip. 'I know we've got to go after him – and it will be easy to find the house. The address was given in every newspaper account, wasn't it? And we'll go – tonight. But let's be practical. We'll need transport – and my car's at the hotel. And you are in no fit condition to come with me while I get it – even if it would be policy to do so. That Inspector may still be batting about somewhere. I hate to leave you, Abigail, but I think what I must do is go and get the car and come back for you. Can you wait here alone while I do? I'll be as fast as I can—'

She shivered and drew closer to him, but then straightened herself and nodded.

'Of course. We'll save time that way. I'll wait here – but you will hurry, Max, won't you? I'm still – rather edgy. Not as frightened as I was, but a bit nervous.'

'Of course, darling.' He bent his head and kissed her gently. 'Of course. Stay in here, and I'll be as quick as I know how to be.'

And gently, he led her back to the couch, and went, closing the door softly behind him, and she listened to his footsteps going down the path, and heard the silence sweep inexorably back. And shivered again, and sat curled up hugging herself to keep the fear at bay.

She used another trick of her childhood as she sat there, choosing a long word – ambulance – and seeing how many smaller words she could make out of the letters in it. She had reached seven, and was trying to follow 'clan' and 'calm' with another beginning with the letter C, when the light from the candlestick on the table suddenly flared, and she turned to look at it.

The stump of candle had burned almost completely away. There was just a pool of wax and a long curled black wick guttering feebly – and not another candle anywhere in sight.

The fear of being left in the dark made her move, made her get up swiftly to start a search of the dresser to see if she could find more, made her move too quickly, for the light sprang high in the draught her movement created, and then died abruptly – and Max had put the matches back in his pocket, she remembered with a sense of panic.

Keep calm, she apostrophised the frightened voice starting again to clamour in her mind. He won't be long – you'll just have to sit here patiently until he comes, and never mind the darkness. Your eyes will soon get used to it—

And then the silence was broken. A distant purring which came closer, turned into a definite buzz – a car's engine. 'Max,' she whispered hopefully – and then relaxed again. It couldn't be Max, not yet. It would take him at least twice as long again to get back to the hotel and then bring the car here. Just a rare vehicle on a quiet road, that would soon pass and take the purring sound of its engine away into the night.

But it didn't. The car stopped, outside the cottage, and the engine shut off sharply. And then, there was a click of a car door, and footsteps coming up the path. And Abigail stood poised beside the couch, rigid with shock. Who was coming into this remote cottage where she was alone and injured and helpless?

CHAPTER SIX

She would never know just how she managed to move but, when the door opened, she found herself, absurdly, stretched out on the floor with her face pressed against the dusty woodrot-smelling floorboards on the far side of the settee. She felt the rush of cold air, felt the movement that came with it, and closed her eyes momentarily, almost praying in her terror.

There was the scrape of a match, and a dim light sprang up. Opening her eyes gingerly, she found she could see under the settee to the doorway. There were legs standing there. A man's legs. He was wearing scuffed suede shoes, and even as she looked at them the man moved forwards, towards the table.

If he comes any closer, he *must* see me, her secret voice shrieked, but then, the match went out, and she heard a whispered curse. After a second he struck another match, and as he did so she remembered the burnt out candle end. Will he see that the wax has recently melted, realize there is someone here? He must – surely he must! And then, whoever he is, he'll look and find me, and—

But apparently he didn't notice. She heard the rustle of paper and realized the match was being held higher, for the light moved upwards, leaving the floor in shadow again. Danny's note – he'd found Danny's note.

Oh God, she thought. Why didn't we keep it, put it in a pocket or something? Whoever this man is, he means trouble, I'm sure of that. Perhaps trouble for Danny, now he's found that note.

Whoever he is? the voice in her mind said. Whoever he is? You know what you think, don't you? You think this is Miles Tenterden. You think this is the man you saw in the square this morning, and that he's Miles Tenterden, that he's looking for Danny – and probably you, too.

The match went out, and after a second of fumbling, another one was struck. And then the paper rustled again, and she heard a soft grunt. Of satisfaction? Possibly. Indeed, probably, for when that match went out, he didn't strike another, but moved back towards the door. It clicked, and again she felt a rush of cold air, again heard footsteps, this time receding along the path. Whatever the man had come for, he'd found it, for he was going away. She heard the gate creak, and suddenly, she felt she had to know, at whatever cost, at whatever risk to herself, just who he was. She *had* to know what he looked like.

She half crawled, half fell across the room to the window, and flattening herself against the wall, looked round the curtain to the path and the gate and roadway beyond. It was dark, but so much darker inside the cottage that she was able to see fairly clearly. There was a small car parked by the gate, and standing in front of it, peering at a map in the beam of the car's riding lights, she could see a man's figure. She couldn't see his face, for his back was to her, but she could see what he was wearing. A pale coloured Burberry. It *was* the man from the square, and she shivered as she looked at him. Was this her husband? It must be, she thought bleakly. Why else should the sight of him so frighten her, why else did he seem familiar to her?

The man moved then, raised his head and came back from the front of the car towards the gate, and for one sick moment she thought he was coming back into the cottage. But he didn't; he climbed into the car, and the engine coughed and purred into life, and the car moved forwards, its red rear lights winking at her above a twisted fender in a sort of triumph. And fear came back, sick and cloying.

He's going to follow Danny, going to catch him and finish the job he started. Unless Danny had a good start, had found a way to get himself safely back to London before his pursuer caught up with him, he was in danger. And only she and Max could help him, only she and Max knew where the danger lay. But Max wasn't here yet. And though he knew they had to get to Danny, he didn't yet know how urgent it had become.

The next half hour crept by like an eternity. She sat by the window peering out in the darkness until her eyes watered with their concentration, stretching her ears to catch every sound that might herald Max's return. And so thrown into despair was she by the long wait that when the estate car did stop at the gate she sat for another second in bemused inactivity before she fully realized that he actually and at last had come back.

She ran out of the cottage and down the path, ignoring the pain in her ankle, and reached it as Max was getting out.

'No – no,' she gasped, pushing him back into the driving seat. 'We haven't a moment to spare – start the engine again—' and she ran round the car to hurl herself into the passenger seat.

'What the hell?—' Max said, but obediently, started the engine and put the car into gear.

'On this road, – it must lead to a main road East, to London – do hurry. You must catch him—'

The car moved forwards and gathered speed, and without taking his eyes from the swathe of headlit road in front of them, Max said 'What's happened?'

Breathlessly, she told him of the cottage's visitor, of the way he had seen the note, and left immediately.

'He – he must be going after Danny. And I'm frightened

for him,' she paused, then, as Max halted at the end of the narrow road, and leaned out in an effort to read the finger post at the corner. After a second, he swung the car to the left, and began to gain speed on the better macadam of the surface, for this road was a much wider and better one.

'Max,' she said. 'Max. I think – I'm not sure, but I think I know who this man is.'

'You recognized him? Max said sharply, turning his glance at her briefly before concentrating again on the dark road flying before them.

'Not exactly. I mean – he was the man I saw in the square this morning. You thought it might be the hotel manager, but it wasn't, I know that now. So, there's only one person it could be,' she swallowed painfully. 'Danny's father.'

'Your husband.'

'Don't call him that!' she said violently.

'But Danny's father is your husband, Abigail. You can't ignore that fact even if you can't remember it. Did – did the sight of this man make you feel anything – anything at all?'

'Frightened,' she said succinctly.

'No, I mean something more than that. Emotional involvement.'

She shook her head with the same violent rejection. 'No! I just felt I knew him from somewhere, and he frightened me. That's all – Oh, Max, I *must* remember soon, mustn't I? How much longer can I go on this state? I feel so stupid, so lost and – and helpless. And I'm not the helpless type, truly I'm not.'

'I don't for one moment think you are. Look, let's forget memory for a while, and use some deduction. As I work it out, you've been a brave sort of person, and far from helpless.'

'How do you mean?'

He settled in his seat as they reached another cross-roads, this time meeting a wide major artery swishing with traffic. They moved into the stream of cars and lorries, and the car built up till it was doing a steady fifty miles an hour, which was pretty good for so ancient a vehicle as the battered estate car. Without for one moment letting his concentration on the road slacken, Max talked.

'From what you've remembered so far, Danny was in some sort of danger. Somebody – a woman – came and told you, and what did you do?'

'I can't *remember*—' she began to feel anger and frustration building in her again.

'Be quiet. What you obviously did, going by your other fragment of recollection, was go and see what was happening. You didn't hide with your head under the blankets. You went and walked into danger, even though you'd been warned there was danger there. That's not being helpless and stupid, is it? Anyway, you got – apparently – a wallop on the head for your brave pains, and hence your present amnesia. The question that is really interesting is – what did you do next?'

'Are you really asking me that? Or is that merely a rhetorical question too?'

He smiled briefly. 'Merely rhetorical. As I see it, what you then did was come round after your wallop, and discover that Danny was alive. Right?'

'He must have been – of course. Why else the note?'

'Why else? I did wonder for a while if the note was genuine—'

She stared at him. 'Of course it was genuine. Why shouldn't it be?'

He shrugged slightly. 'It might have been a planted thing – part of some mad complicated plot I don't understand yet. But now I'm sure it's genuine, because that

man – whoever he is – and we still don't know – took it
seriously. He accepted it as genuine, because he went belting off as soon as he saw it, didn't he? Anyway, the note
proves Danny is still alive, which brings us to the next
deduction. That you took Danny to that cottage.'

She frowned, trying to sort it all out. 'Because I knew
the cottage – knew where it was?'

'Precisely. I wish you could remember *how* you knew
it—'

An oncoming lorry had its headlights thrown instead
of dipped, so the car suddenly filled with blazing light.
Automatically, Abigail closed her eyes against the glare,
and in the yellow-black murk behind her lids, heard her
own voice say with a sort of impatience 'Because I'd
bought it—'

The light disappeared as the lorry went roaring past,
and she heard Max say softly above the noise of their own
engine, 'When did you buy it? Why?'

With her eyes still closed, Abigail said, with a momentary return to that now familiar dreamlike state 'It was to
be a surprise. He had so much more money than me, you
see. But I had a little. And I wanted to buy something
myself – and the cottage, when I saw a picture of it at
the estate agent's, looked so pretty—'

Her eyes snapped open, and she twisted in her seat and
stared at Max with excitement surging up in her. 'Max –
I've remembered something else, haven't I?'

'Indeed you have – can you add to it at all?' He
manoeuvred the car skilfully, pulling out to overtake
another lumbering lorry doing a rumbling thirty miles
an hour in front of them. She wrinkled her eyes, trying
to catch hold of that momentary picture she had had of
herself, sitting at an estate agent's desk and looking at a
photograph of the cottage, and then another vision of
herself walking up the path, on a sunlit afternoon.

The remembered pictures were superimposed on the reality of the road before them and on the right there was a brightly lit forecourt, in front of a transport café, with cars and lorries parked in serried ranks. As Max drove past, the memories after which she was groping disappeared as suddenly as they had arisen, because she saw something far more important.

'Max!' she cried, turning in her seat to peer back over her shoulder at the café – 'Max – stop!'

Immediately, he stood on the brakes, and the car shrieked to a standstill on the soft shoulder of the road.

'What's the matter – what have you remembered?'

She shook her head. 'No – it's not that. It's what I just *saw*. The man. I just saw his car at the transport café – I'm sure it was. It had a twisted rear fender, and I recognized it.'

'Then we'd better look,' Max said practically, and put the car into reverse gear.

'No – no we mustn't – we've got to get on – but at least we've caught up with him, and now we can get ahead of him—'

But Max was turning the car, and driving back the few hundred yards to the café.

'We've got to be sure. It won't take long to make certain. Until we know where he is, we're in a fool's paradise.'

He stopped the car short of the brightly lit forecourt, so that they could just see the parked vehicles, and see into the café through its big glass windows, blazing with light.

'I'm sure that's the car,' Abigail whispered. 'That one there,' and she pointed. 'I only saw it once, but that fender looked so – sort of drunk in my mind's eye.'

She looked beyond the car, parked quietly beside a big lorry, at the windows of the café, and then clutched Max's arm.

'It is – it is! Look! He's in there – by the window at one of the tables. The man in the pale coloured raincoat. See him?'

Max peered and said 'Where?' but even as he spoke, another lorry pulled across the forecourt and stopped in front of the café windows.

'Oh *hell*' Abigail said. 'Hell, hell, *hell*! You can't see him now – but it was him, truly—'

'Sitting eating, you say?'

'Yes – and—'

'That settles it then. I'm going in there.'

'What for? We've got to get on now – ahead of him.'

He shook his head and said quickly 'No. Listen Abigail. It would be better to *follow* him. He's the man we think is after Danny. Well, we've got a better chance of keeping Danny safe if we keep this bloke right under our eyes, haven't we? And there's another point. You need some food – yes,' he put his hand over her mouth as she opened it to protest. 'Yes, you do. I'm going in there to buy some sandwiches and a drink we can take here in the car. And then when Pale Raincoat leaves, we follow. No arguments,' and he leaned forward and kissed her briefly, and slid out of the car.

Anxiously she watched him go, and then almost leapt out of the car after him. For, just as Max disappeared from her sight behind the lorry parked by the entrance, the man in the pale raincoat appeared on the other side, buttoning his coat and pulling up his collar, making purposefully for his car with the twisted fender. It was as pat as a tightly rehearsed scene from a French farce, and she could have screamed with the urgency of the need to call Max back.

But she couldn't get out of the car, couldn't call Max back, for if she had, the raincoated man would have seen her, and she knew with every fibre of her being that that would mean danger.

Helplessly she watched him get into his car, heard his engine start, praying wordlessly for Max to come back, *now*, before the man could get away.

The car with the twisted fender began to move, and almost without thinking of what she was doing, Abigail slid across into the driver's seat, and turned the ignition key. The car coughed, and settled to a steady purr, and she put it into first gear.

As the other car moved round in a wide sweep to leave the forecourt, she twisted hard on the steering wheel, and turned her own vehicle in a tight circle, so that as the man in the raincoat drove past her, she was pointing the bonnet in the same direction.

'Forgive me Max, dear Max – forgive me,' she muttered feverishly, as she peered anxiously through the windscreen. 'I need you, and I'm scared, but I can't let him get away, can I? I've got to stop him from getting to Danny – I've got to—'

And she slid the car into top gear, and settled more firmly into her seat, with her eyes fixed on the red rear lights of the car with the twisted fender, running ahead of her into – what?

CHAPTER SEVEN

She felt like someone in limbo. There was the dim glow from the dashboard of the car, her own headlights sweeping and dancing on the dark road in front of her, and the winking red lights of the car ahead. It wasn't too difficult to keep up with him, for he drove at a steady forty miles an hour, and was an unadventurous driver. Where Abigail would have overtaken, had she been leading instead of following, he drove sedately behind lorries and slow cars. But she wasn't sorry. Fatigue had entered into her very bones, making her ache horribly, making her knees and thighs tremble, so that when she had to change gear, she did so noisily, so difficult was it to manipulate clutch and accelerator smoothly. And her eyes – her eyes were hot and sandy, red rimmed from exhaustion, she knew, almost as painful as her ankle, which had settled into a deep sick nagging moan of misery.

Her mind wandered too, as the time crept by and they drove on and on. While part of her was occupied with the concentration necessary to keep the car in front in sight but not so close that she would be noticed by the driver, the rest of her buzzed and twisted and shouted and whispered, conjecture, fear, doubt, helpless anger, all battling inside her tired aching head. There was a brief moment when she thought in sudden terror – where am I? where am I going? I don't know. I'm going to drive right off the edge of the world, soon, and no one, no one at all will ever know what happened, and I'll never see Max again.

But the thought of Max steadied her. She conjured up a vision of him standing dour and scowling by the notice board at the hotel, all those aeons ago, and wondered how she could ever have been frightened of him. Dear comfortable Max, who seemed to find her as special as she found him.

But the traitorous secret voice that lay lurking there in the deepest recesses of her mind started up again.

Does he? Does he really? In spite of all those doubts he has about your story?

He *hasn't* any doubts, she argued back. None at all. If he had, he wouldn't be helping me this way—

Helping you? No doubts? Come off it. Remember what he said? That he's wondered whether the note Danny left was genuine? Remember the way he insisted on going into the café? Was that being all that helpful, when what you wanted to do was to get to Danny, *fast*! How helpful was that? Look at you now – on your own, after a dangerous man, and no helpful Max around.

She almost pleaded with herself, in this odd ding-dong argument between the two parts of her own personality. But why? she asked that teasing suspicious other half why should he latch onto me as he did if it wasn't that he *really* wanted to help?

Because maybe he's part of the mess himself. Maybe he's in with the man in the pale raincoat, maybe that's why he was so anxious to get into the café after him. And what about that note from Danny? Remember? 'She can always ask M who likes me I think though like I said I like you better than both of them.' Remember that? *Who is M?* Couldn't it be this very Max you've let yourself get so besotted with? Can't you see that maybe you're in more danger from your precious Max than from Tenterden?—

'No, no, *no!*' and she whispered it aloud, so that the sounds bounced back at her from the windscreen. That can't be true. If I hadn't seen the car parked at that café,

75

he'd never have stopped, so that isn't on – And as for the M in the note – that could be anyone – a woman even. It just isn't *on*—

All right then. The police. He's police, and he's latched on to you just to lead you on and collect evidence before hauling you into court – remember the way he talked to that Inspector? They didn't sound as though he were a stranger, did it? The way he talked – it was as though he were *taking* the initiative, not as though he was simply answering questions the way you thought he was, the way he told you—

I'm not going to listen any more, she told the insistent little voice firmly. Shut up, do you hear? I'm not going to think about Max, or the whys and wherefores of him, not now. All that matters now is getting Danny out of trouble.

And the memory of that dark curly head, that battered small face came up before her strained and watery red eyes, and effectively drowned the little voice.

They must have been a bare ten miles or so from the outer ring of London suburbs when she nearly came to the end of her chase in ignominy. The car she was following suddenly disappeared. It had been in front of her for miles, those red rear lights so imprinted on her vision that she could have seen them with her eyes closed. And suddenly they just weren't there.

She leaned forwards and stared out into the thick darkness, quiet, because in the small hours as it now was the traffic had dwindled to a mere trickle of London bound lorries. She kept the car moving, in a low gear, and it was probably because it was idling along that it happened – and saved her.

The engine suddenly stalled, as her trembling foot slipped on the clutch – but the car was on an incline, and silently it went on moving forwards. She was too bemused

76

to put her foot on the brake, and as she reached for the ignition key to restart the engine, she noticed two things.

First, that her petrol gauge was pointing to almost empty. That was shocking enough. And secondly, that just as she was about to put her foot on the brake to stop the slow rolling of the car, it slid past a layby – in which was parked the car with the twisted fender.

It was almost miraculous, she thought, trembling with reaction. If the petrol hadn't almost run out, the car probably wouldn't have stalled, and if it hadn't stalled I would have driven right past Pale Raincoat and not noticed him – and lost him. It *is* a miracle, so help me.

About fifty yards beyond the layby, the incline levelled out and the car slowed agonizingly and finally stopped. She sat there for a while, listening, but clearly the other car wasn't leaving its parking place. And now what, she asked herself bleakly? Stuck nowhere with no petrol at all? An obliging quarry, undoubtedly, sitting there waiting for me, but where do we go from here?

Look for petrol, idiot, the little voice advised. This is an estate car with a big boot – maybe there's a can of extra petrol in it.

There was. She got out of the car quietly, and though she almost fell when she tried to stand up, her legs were so shaky and weary, she managed to creep to the rear of the car. The boot wasn't locked – and there *was* a can of petrol.

It took an eternity to find the cap of the car's tank, to empty the petrol from the spare can into it, biting her lips in case the car now behind her should start to move again, but she managed it, and still there was no sound in the darkness, only the occasional roaring grumble of a passing lorry – and there were only two of them.

She stood half leaning on the car when she had replaced the empty can in the boot, and considered her next step.

And had to dig up all her shredded courage to do what she decided was best.

Moving like a cat in the shadows of the hedge, she made her way back along the road towards the layby. I've got to see what's going on, haven't I? she told herself. No sense sitting chewing my nails and not knowing—

He lay back in his seat, his head sprawling sideways, his mouth hanging open in an unlovely grimace. For one sick moment she thought he was dead, but then she saw his chest move and understood. He was asleep.

She stood in the shadow of a hawthorn and looked at him, but he was deeply asleep, she could see even from this distance.

A sensible man, remarked her secret voice. He's grabbing some much needed rest. Why don't you? You might as well, though if you've any sense at all you'll drive to the nearest police station and let them handle the whole sorry mess—

'Like hell I will,' she whispered in answer. 'Like hell I will. I'll just wait till he wakes up and goes on—'

And she crept back to the estate car, and settled herself in the driver's seat again to wait as patiently as she could.

And of course the private argument with herself started up again, over and over again, the fears and doubts, the sick nagging about Miles Tenterden, the wondering about Max's motives – but still, stubborn in her fatigue, she stuck to her essential belief. The only thing that mattered was Danny. Whatever Max was or wasn't, who-ever the man behind her was or wasn't, Danny had to be found and protected. And she also clung to her con-viction planted in her by Max – that as long as the man be-hind her was followed, Danny was safe.

The night thickened and darkened even more, if that were possible, and she wondered stupidly what the time was. Darkest before dawn, isn't it? she asked the little secret voice, but there was no help to be found there any more, for the other part of her mind seemed to have shut up shop, to have opted out of the whole mess—

She awoke abruptly just as the car with the twisted rear fender passed. She was lying sprawled sideways, across the passenger seat, and as she sat awkwardly upright fumbling for the ignition key, she realized that it was this that had probably saved her from detection. Her car must have looked empty as Pale Raincoat went by. Another miniature miracle.

The darkness was thinning out, now, not that there was any real light in the sky. It was as though a couple of layers of chiffon had been drawn back, so the darkness lost some of its stifling velvety quality. Now there was a promise of light to come, some time soon.

And the landscape changed too. Fields and hedges gave way to scattered houses; the houses closed up, become strings of semi detached villas sitting prim and complacent in miniscule front gardens. There were cars parked on grassy verges and against the edges of the pavements that now fringed the wide road and this helped her keep Twisted Fender in sight without being seen herself.

And now, suddenly, fear and depression settled over her like a pall. They were so nearly at the end of the journey, and for the first time, she started to think about what she would do when eventually Pale Raincoat stopped, and left the car. Would she just park behind him, leap out and say 'Stop! You shall go no further!'? That would be ludicrous. Follow him on foot? To where?

I don't know, the little voice said sourly, suddenly waking up again. Where do you think he's going?

To the house, she answered. To the house I remembered with such terror. I can't follow him into there—

But I'll have to. I've come this far. If he does go into

79

the house. I can't just stand skulking on the pavement outside while he goes in and finishes off the job he started on Danny.

But how are you going to get into the house, idiot? came the hateful little voice. Use some sense, woman. Get the police, get them to help you – you can't do it alone.

But will they believe me? Max said they'd just arrest me, and that wouuld be that – and I believe him. I *do* believe him, I believe everything he said.

Do you? retorted the little voice. Of course you don't. This is me you're arguing with, me who is really you—

A set of traffic lights winked lollipop green and then amber in front of her, and changed to a firm red before she could shoot over the crossing. The rear lights of the car she was following dwindled and disappeared far in front of her, and as she reluctantly stopped the car at the row of studs that edged the crossing, she stared after it anxiously – and then turned her head as another vehicle drew alongside.

A policeman on a motor scooter. Instinctively she slid down a little in her seat, but he didn't turn his head, gazing blankly ahead of him at the lights, yawning hugely.

She stared at him, fascinated. They say you're getting old when policemen start to look young, and this one looks very boyish under that absurd helmet of his, with peach-down cheeks and rather slight shoulders. Shall I wind down the window and lean out and say – 'will you help me? You're looking for me in connection with the disappearance of my stepson, but never mind that – will you help me? I'm chasing the man who really hurt Danny.' And what will he say? 'Well, now, Madam, how do you know he's at all involved? Who is he? You'd better come along with me—' I can't do that.

But I'm so tired, and so frightened. Wouldn't it be

better to let them put me in a cell and let me sleep and leave them to get on with the hunting of Danny, the protection of him? And the thought of sleeping, even in a cell on a hard pallet, was so suddenly enticing that she put out her hand to open the window.

But the lights winked amber and green again, and the motor scooter moved forwards and turned right, and that was that. As her own car crossed the intersection she looked after the little figure, so absurdly perched on its Noddy scooter, with a sort of longing – but it was too late now.

She increased her speed anxiously. She was still committed to her chase, but where was her quarry? He'd had time to make half a dozen turns; perhaps she had lost him for good and all.

But there ahead was another set of traffic lights just turning to green and as she came up to them she saw the car with the twisted fender draw away, gather speed and then turn left. And she followed.

They reached a big complex of roads, a roundabout heralded by a confusion of blue and yellow signs, and she thought – Chiswick Flyover – not far now – and was jolted as she realized she knew the house was only a bare half hour away now. Kensington! crowed the little voice. It's in Kensington, remember?

If you say so, she told it. If you remember it it's the same as me remembering it, because all you are is another part of me – and then she giggled aloud. I must be tired, to behave in so schizophrenic a fashion, talking to my voices. I'll be thinking I'm Joan of Arc next – or is that paranoia? Hell, *I* don't know.

She followed the other car round the curl of the roundabout, up the steep little exit road signed 'Central London' and realized she would find it much harder now to keep him in sight. The traffic had thickened noticeably, clotting into groups of private cars as well as lorries, with well-lit lumbering red buses careering serenely along on the crown of the road, cutting off her forward vision almost completely.

'What you need for a quick getaway is our motor oil—' read the advertisement on the rear of the bus behind which she was dodging irritably. What I need is a quick get-away period – she told it, and as it drew in to a stopping place slid past.

She could just see the car she was following, and even as she spotted it turning right, the rear lights winked out. Almost surprised, she realized that dawn had arrived, a grey dawn that held a faint rosiness in it, lighting the sky above the jagged edges of the rooftops with a promise of sunshine to come.

They were away from the heavy traffic now, in roads lined with tall narrow houses, and curbs tightly edged with parked cars. Colour had arrived with the dawn, and she could see winking yellow daffodils in window boxes, the fat blue and white spears of hyacinths, the tender young green of plane trees, and her heart lifted a little in spite of her fatigue. Whatever happens to individuals, life goes on, she told herself philosophically. If we're all dead and forgotten this time tomorrow, those hyacinths will still be lacing the air with their scent—

The car ahead slowed down, and automatically she slid her foot onto the clutch, dropping back a little. It turned right yet again, and slowly, with a new surge of fear in her belly she followed.

They were in a broad square, lined with tall houses with heavy porticoes in front of them and the delicate iron fretwork of balconies above, frowning down on a central railing-enclosed green patch.

Still there were the ubiquitous parked cars, and as she slid the nose of the estate car into the centre of the road, the quarry could be seen backing into an empty space on the garden side.

Moving with a smoothness that amazed her, she stopped the car, put it into reverse, and curled back round the corner, and then chose first gear again, and went across the right hand entry to the square, and round it, so that she traversed three sides of it before coming again into the side where the car with the twisted fender had parked.

There was a space – a very small one – on the corner on the garden side, and she inched the car into it, and turned off the engine. And as she did, she saw him.

He was crossing the road, unbuttoning his raincoat as he went, and as he pushed between two cars, he pulled it off, tossing it over one arm. He crossed the pavement purposefully, and ran up the steps of a house painted in white, which made it stand out from its neighbours, disappearing into the shadows of the portico which overhung the front door.

I'm glad I chose white paint, Abigail thought, and was jolted again by her capricious memory. She could see herself talking to a man in blue overalls, hear her own voice. 'I know white gets dirty quickly in London, but it would look so fresh and hopeful, wouldn't it?' and he had grinned and said 'All right, lady. It's your money—'

Stiffly, she got out of the car, and tried to straighten her clothes as she stood beside it, grimacing ruefully as she saw for the first time how she looked. The black skirt and jacket were more than horribly creased; they were smeared with mud and grass stains. Her stockings were torn and her skin grazed and crusted with dried blood from scratches, and her shoes, those elegant high heeled black shoes, would never look decent again, however carefully they were cleaned. God knows what my face and hair look like, she thought, and with a sudden gesture pulled the few remaining hair pins from the back of her head, so that her hair swung down into its usual swathes on each side of her face.

Almost on tiptoe, she moved along the pavement, with the parked cars between her and the road until she was opposite the white painted house. And then she shrank back against the glossy black railings, and stared hard at the front of it.

The windows looked blank, drawn curtains at all of them, and she could just see the heavy closed front door in its shadowed porch. There was no sign of life at all, and as she leaned on the hardness of the railings, her thoughts became woolly again.

Now what do I do? she asked herself. Wait here? Or go in? And if I go in, what then?

Don't ask me, came the little voice in prompt reply. Don't ask me—

And then she saw it. High up, at the top level of windows, just beneath the steep pitch of the black soot-encrusted roof, there was a small window, curtained like all the others. And it was there she saw movement. The curtain trembled, slid to one side, and even as she stared a white blur appeared in the black gap left by the movement of the curtain. A face – a small face. It peered out, and then, as abruptly as it had appeared, was gone, the curtain sliding back into place.

'Danny!' she said it aloud, staring up at the window with straining eyes, but there was no more movement, none at all.

That does it, she thought. That definitely does it. Danny's in there, and that man has gone in too. Unless I stop him he'll do something to the child, and I'm not going to stand out here like a useless piece of furniture and let him get away with it. I'm going in.

And lifting her head, she limped across the square, between the cars, and climbed the steps of the house. And without looking for it, reached for the bell pull she knew was at the right hand side, while she stared at the blue and red stained glass set into the heavy door.

CHAPTER EIGHT

She heard the bell pealing hoarsely, a long way inside the house, and shivered a little. I don't know what I'm going to say to whoever answers – but here I am, and here I stay. No turning back now.

There was a long pause, and she rang again, and as the peal died away, she heard it. Shuffling footsteps, coming nearer. Through the stained glass inserts in the door she could see a distorted shadow coming closer, and her heart thudded thickly in her chest. The shadow stopped just on the other side of the door, but made no attempt to open it, and again Abigail pulled on the doorbell.

And, this time, there were sounds as the door fastening was fumbled with on the other side, and slowly the door opened a small fraction.

It opened very slowly indeed, and Abigail leaned forwards and pushed on it. Through the crack that showed at the side, a pale blur appeared, became a face. A woman's face.

'Who is it? Who's there?' the woman said in a sibilant whisper, and irritably, Abigail pushed on the door again, with a show of courage she was far from feeling.

'It's me – Abigail' she said, and then the door opened widely, and she was inside.

A woman in a dull green dressing gown, with the collar pulled up and held about her scrawny neck with defensive hands stood staring at her with her mouth open. And as she looked at the thin face, petulant under its untidy brown hair, Abigail remembered.

'Cecily,' she said. 'Cecily. It's only me – Abigail. Don't look like that—'

'Abigail?' the woman said, stupidly. *'Abigail?'*

Yes,' Abigail said, gently, for the woman look dumb-founded. 'Don't be frightened, Cecily, I'm all right. He didn't kill me, any more than he killed Danny – though he tried hard enough—'

And after a moment in which she went on staring at Abigail with a sort of imbecile amazement, the woman hurled herself at the girl, threw her arms round her and burst into tears.

'Oh, Thank God you're safe – Thank God – I thought—'

Gently, Abigail disentangled herself, and pushed the other woman away. 'Come and sit down, Cecily,' she said, and obediently, Cecily sank down on the heavy maho-gany seat under the hall stand.

Abigail lifted her head and looked around her, and felt a deep sense of familiarity as she did so. A narrow hall, floored in squares of black and white. Heavy dark red wallpaper, thickly covered with pictures so dark with ancient varnish the subjects couldn't be seen. Heavy oak doors lining the hallway, and a flight of red carpeted stairs going upwards into a gloom lit with patches of blue and red light from the front door. This is the house, she thought drearily. This is the house.

Then she turned back to Cecily, sitting hunched up on the hall settle staring up at her with a look of bemused anxiety on her lined face.

'Where is he – the man I followed here?'

'The man you followed here?' Cecily said sharply, her face showing a sudden surprise.

'I haven't time now to explain properly,' Abigail said wearily. 'But my memory's gone all – peculiar. I know I know him, but I don't know who he is. I just followed him here – and I saw him come into the house. Where is

87

he? And where's Danny? It *was* his face I saw at the window wasn't it?'

Cecily stared at her again, and then said, almost wonderingly, 'But there's no one here but me and Danny – no man – who was it?'

'I told you – I don't *know*,' Abigail said, dropping her voice to a whisper. 'I followed him here, and he came into the house – I saw him.'

Fear sprang up in the other woman's face, and she got to her feet, poised as for flight. 'I heard no one come in, Abigail – oh God, has he come back? Is he here in the house, and I didn't hear him come in?'

'*I don't know*,' Abigail said again. 'Listen, Cecily – *was* it Danny I saw at the window upstairs?'

The other woman nodded. 'I hid him – he got here in the small hours – he said he'd got a lift in a lorry, and I hid him upstairs – in case Miles came back and found him – I'm so frightened of him, Abby, so frightened.

'That's why I didn't dare tell the police what really happened here that night, in case Miles tried to kill me too, when the police had gone away—'

'He – Miles, was *here* that night?' Abigail stared at her, her head spinning with shock. 'Not abroad? I had the idea that he'd had to be sent for from abroad – *afterwards*—'

'Don't you remember?' Cecily peered at her in the dim red and blue light, her face ludicrously banded with the reflected colours. 'Don't you remember? I came to your room, and I told you – I'd seen Miles come in, and heard him with Danny – and I was frightened for Danny, so I came and told you and you went down to see—' tears began to trickle down her face 'and you went down – and then Miles hurt you too—' and she began to weep helplessly.

Abigail stared at her, and then leaned forwards and took her shoulders and shook her. 'But what happened *afterwards*? What? You've got to tell me.'

Cecily shook her head, and gulped sickeningly. 'I don't know,' she said piteously. 'I don't *know*. I was – so frightened. I – hid in my room, all night, and in the morning, it was all quiet – and I – I came down, and you were gone, you and Danny – and the drawing room was all — and then Miles came in the front door, and said he'd just come back from France, and I didn't dare say I knew he'd been here the night before – I didn't dare – I thought he'd – killed both of you, and then got rid of your – your bodies. And he called the police and I didn't tell them what really happened – I didn't dare, Abby. You know I'm a frightened woman – I just couldn't tell them – Abby, don't hate me for being frightened!'

And even though she kept her voice to a whisper, there was a thick layer of hysteria in Cecily, a tenseness that Abigail could feel like a tangible thing. She stared at the dressing gowned shape, at the haggard weak face, and a brief disgusted anger rose in her, giving her a new strength. Frightened as she was herself, weak as she was herself, she still wasn't as useless as this trembling weeping piece of humanity.

'I'm not angry – but we can't waste time. Miles is in this house somewhere. He can't have heard us, or surely he'd be here by now? The doorbell though, maybe—'

'The milkman usually rings at about this time—' Cecily said.

'Thank God for that – he must have thought – look, Cecily, we've got to get Danny out of here, fast, and to the police where he'll be safe, before Miles gets at him – where is he?'

'Miles?' Cecily said stupidly.

Abigail could have hit her. 'No – *Danny*!' And then a

sudden thought stopped her. 'Cecily – what does Miles look like?'

Cecily had started to move towards the stairs, but at this she turned and stared. 'Look like? Your own *husband*? Why ask that?'

'Because I can't remember him,' Abigail said with a spurt of anger. And then added wearily 'Oh, forget it, it doesn't matter. There isn't time now. I just don't know who that man was I followed here. But it must be Miles. I did recognize him, I suppose – in a way.'

She began to follow Cecily who had turned again to the stairs, and then said suddenly, as another thought hit her 'Look, Cecily – who is M?'

'M? What do you mean?'

'A note Danny wrote – he mentioned an M.'

'Well – Miles I suppose – oh, Abigail—' Cecily turned back from the bottom step. 'Abby – is he really in the house? I'm so frightened, Abby. I've locked myself in ever since it happened. I only let the police in – and I couldn't tell them about it in case Miles came back again—'

'But you said he *had* come back—' Abigail said, her head swimming as she tried to sort out the sequence of events, tried to make what Cecily was saying fit in with her scraps of memory.

'Oh he did – but after the police had finished and all, he went away again. He told the police he was going to find his boy and find you, and just went, and I've been so afraid he'd come back. That's why I locked myself in, why I was so scared when Danny let himself in last night. I heard the key, and thought it was Miles, but it was just Danny, so I hid him, and locked us in again – and oh, I should have told the police, I know I should but I couldn't. I told you, Abby – I'm—'

'I know,' Abigail said tartly. 'I know. You're a

frightened woman. Look, we've got to get Danny *out* of here. We can't talk any more now – Miles is here in this house somewhere and we've all three of us got to get out – where's Danny—?'

Heavily Cecily began to climb the stairs, and Abigail followed her. As they moved upwards, creeping, Cecily whispered over her shoulder 'I put him in the attic – in case Miles came back and looked in his bedroom. I knew Miles must know he wasn't dead, you see – once Danny came here last night, it all made sense. Miles must have known he was alive still and gone to find him to – to kill him properly—'

'But why didn't you call the police then when Danny came back?' Abigail hissed at her. 'You had enough proof to get their protection, for God's sake!'

'I was frightened,' Cecily said, with a sort of dreary persistence. 'I was frightened—'

The first landing was dark and smelled heavily of polish and dust, and as they passed one of the dark closed doors Abigail thought with a start – that's my bedroom. But they went past, to a second flight of stairs, linoleum covered this time, not carpeted.

There was yet another flight of stairs to go up, and as they reached the second landing, Abigail stopped for breath, for complete exhaustion was hovering very close now. And thought she heard something. A scratching sound.

'Listen,' she whispered, putting a hand on Cecily's shoulder. And they both stood immobile, straining to hear. But there was just an ear-ringing silence broken only by distant sounds of traffic from the road far below.

'Abigail – what was it?' Cecily hissed, and Abigail could feel her trembling under her hand.

'I don't know – whatever it was, it's stopped now. Come on – where is he?'

'The far attic,' whispered Cecily, and clung to Abigail's hand with a dry chill grasp as they moved on and up the stairs.

It was very dark on the landing, and Abigail fell back as Cecily fumbled with one of the doors. Then, she pushed it open, and looked over her shoulder at Abigail.

Eagerly, Abigail pushed forwards, and hurried past her into the room beyond, a room filled with the thin yellow light of early morning sunshine.

'Danny? Danny?—' she said breathlessly – and then whirled. For the door slammed shut behind her, and she heard the rattle of the tumblers as the key was turned in the lock. Furiously she hurled herself at the door, and shouted – 'Cecily! What the hell are you doing? Cecily—'

'You bloody little idiot!' Cecily's voice came shrilly from beyond the door. 'You bloody little *fool*. Letting him lead you back here like a lamb to the slaughter. If you'd had the sense to keep away, you'd be *alive*, you hear me? This way you're dead, dead, dead, *dead*—' and she laughed again, sick and shrill.

'Shut up, Cisse!' At the sound of the deep note of a man's voice, Abigail stopped banging on the door, stopped shaking on the handle, and listened, frozen with shock.

'Shut *up*,' the man said again, his voice a little muffled by the heavy door. 'Crowing like some farmyard hen isn't going to help one bit—'

But Cecily only laughed again, and the door rattled as she did. She was banging on it with a sort of triumphant drum-beat, Abigail realized.

'But I'm enjoying myself,' she cried. 'Enjoying myself, you hear me, Madam High and Mighty Jumped-Up Abigail? Thought you'd rob me, did you, rob me of my rights in that boy? Thought you'd get him to love a stepmother more than his own aunt, his own flesh and blood? Thought you'd get his money for yourself, did you? Not enough for you to get a wedding ring, was it? Had to have it all, didn't you? Well, you've *got* it all, Madam Stupid, you've got it all – and much good may it do you – you hear me? Much good may—'

There was a sharp sound, and Abigail heard Cecily draw a sharp hissing breath.

He's slapped her, she thought. Slapped her – who has slapped her? Miles?

She hurled herself at the door again, but it held fast, and beyond it she heard footsteps, and another peal of that sick laughter, and she stood very still, her ear pressed against the panels, trying to hear what was happening. The footsteps dwindled, softened in sound, and then there was just silence. A thick silence that was like a blanket.

She stood for another interminable minute listening, and was just about to draw a breath to shout again, when she did hear something.

At first, she thought it was an animal crying somewhere, so high and plaintive was the sound but then she listened again, and knew.

It was a child crying, crying in long piteous moans, and in an agony of frustration, Abigail ran about the room, banging on the walls, throwing aside the few broken chairs and the battered card table which were its only furniture, seeking a way out. The child cried again, remote and with such misery and fear in the sound that Abigail beat her own forehead with her fists and cried out aloud.

'Danny – Danny – I'm trying – I'm trying – I will come, I will – Danny!—'

And she ran back to the door and again beat against it till her hands bled and the pain forced her to stop.

And again that plaintive cry filled her ears, and this time she ran to the window. It was locked, but the panes were broad and with a strength she didn't know she had, she seized one of the chairs and swung it widely and hit the glass with a tinkling jangling curiously satisfying crash.

Recklessly, she thrust with her elbow at the fragments of stiletto sharp glass still clinging to the edges of the window frame, and looked out. Far below her the road with its parked cars lay serene and still in the brilliance of the early May sunshine, but not a person was in sight. Only a solitary black cat stalked in foreshortened long legged dignity across the central garden. No one to answer a call for help. No one at all.

And again she heard it, that high pleading cry, and again the agony of being locked up and frustrated almost overcame her, so that she lifted her head and wept aloud, tears running down her face unheeded.

But gradually, her panic and anger subsided, and thought came to take over, to fill her shaking body with determination. For the next time the child called out, Abigail moved purposefully and swung her legs out through the gap she had made in the dusty window. Somehow she managed to turn her body, so that she hung by her weary hands, with her face pressed against the grimy brickwork, her feet scrabbling for the foothold of a ledge she had seen a few feet below the window.

It was the right side of her face that was against the wall, and she could just see, distorted because only one eye was able to see clearly, a diagonal rail of iron. One of the struts of the balcony, she thought. One of the struts. If I can reach it I can slide down, and get in at the window below. And find Danny and get him out of here. Find Danny and get him out of here.

Her feet found the ledge, and slipped, and for one sick moment she thought she was going to fall – and then the third miracle happened. One of the shoes she should have

94

taken off first hooked itself against the wall, and one convulsive kick sent it spinning off her foot. But her toes were free, and she was able to use them to cling to the ledge.

Gingerly, she moved her hands, one over the other, until she was right at the far edge of the window frame. There was nothing else to hold onto, nothing between her and the diagonal of the balcony. She let go with her left hand, and reached for it, but it was just a few inches beyond her eagerly groping finger tips. The only way she would be able to reach it would be to let go the little support she had. She would have to hurl herself bodily at that metal pole, hoping to catch it, hoping it would take her weight if she did.

And then it became definitely the only thing she could do, for even as she tried to measure the distance with her eye, the piece of the ledge on which her shoeless foot was clinging gave way, and she *had* to let go and throw herself at the only hope of support there was.

With a convulsive movement she closed her eyes, and let go, felt herself fall sideways and downwards, sickeningly.

CHAPTER NINE

The jerk made her retch, closing her throat with a sick clutch that took her breath away. But she clung as instinctively as a young animal clings to its mother's fur. And when she opened her eyes, she was swinging from arms which were convulsively looped round the metal diagonal of the balcony.

All she had to do now was loosen her grip very slightly, to allow her body to slide down the pole to safety of the balcony ten feet or so below – but she couldn't. Anticlimax had hit like a physical blow, and her arms were held in a spasm of muscular contraction that was agonizingly painful. It was as though she had hung there all her life, and would hang there for another eternity, doomed for ever to a peculiar and private hell of her own.

And then, absurdly, she sneezed. That spasm seemed to loosen the one in her arms, for she slid, swinging awkwardly from side to side, until she found herself bent double over the balcony railings which trembled and rocked under her weight.

Somehow she managed to pull herself back, managed to get her feet on the concrete of the balcony floor, and then she was sitting huddled in a corner of it, her hands screaming with pain, her chest torn with the huge retching gulping breaths she had to take.

To sneeze. To hang in mid-air from a slender metal pole, and sneeze herself to safety. It was crazy, so crazy that she started to laugh weakly and helplessly, feeling tears streak through the filth that caked her face, making her breathe even more deeply as she struggled to regain her equilibrium.

To sneeze – why should anyone want to sneeze when she was in imminent danger of a very bloody, ugly death, when nothing but a metal pole stood between her and the hard body-shattering pavement so far below?

The smoke. That was why. The thick smell of smoke. Abigail lifted her head and dragged herself upright, and clung swaying to the balcony railing, staring up at the face of the house. All she could see were the flat curtained windows, curiously foreshortened because of the angle at which she had to look at them. She looked behind her, and down, dizzily, but there was no indication of a source of the smell that had thickened in her nose to that saving sneeze. And words slid into her mind, made her giggle and speak aloud.

'An olfactory hallucination,' she informed the balcony solemnly and giggled again, a little hysterically.

But there was no time for thinking about what had happened, only what had still to happen if she was to get Danny safely out of the house. She stood still for a second, listening, but there was no high pitched cry of a child to be heard – and somehow the silence seemed even more ominous than the cries had done, made it even more imperative that she find him.

Once more she peered over the edge of the balcony, across the square, but there was no one, not so much as the prowling cat to prove she was still in a world full of living creatures. No help anywhere; she was still out on this limb on her own.

She turned to the window that fronted the balcony, and with an automatic movement that had no real hope in it, pulled on the catch that, when released, would let the window swing open. It turned smoothly in her fingers, and she was so startled when in fact it opened, that she stumbled backwards, and fell hard against the cruel edge of the railings, making them sway, so that for one sick moment she thought she would be pitched down into the street after all.

But she recovered, and moving awkwardly round the open half of the window, pushed the heavy dust-smelling curtains aside, and stepped into the room beyond.

It was dark, heavily dark, and she held the curtain high as she looked round. She was in a bedroom, a room with a heavy brass railed bedstead, dark mahogany wardrobes and dressing table, a deep red carpet. Obviously it was not a room that was used for the bed was humped with folded blankets and pillows under a crimson silky counterpane.

The door was opposite the window, and letting the curtain go, she stumbled across the darkened room towards it. If it were locked? What then?

But it wasn't, and she turned the knob very gently, fear coming back in a tidal wave. Her captors were still in the house. It was pretty remarkable they hadn't yet heard her for she must have made a great deal of noise getting out of that attic room. So she moved as gently as she could, and slid out of the dark bedroom into the corridor.

She was on the same floor as the room she had remembered was her own bedroom. She recognized the arrangement of doors, the opening to the flight of linoleum covered stairs that led to the floor above, to which she had so trustingly allowed herself to be led by Cecily. And she stood, very quietly, again listening.

And this time, she realized she had not had an hallucination out there on the balcony. Her nose had reacted to a real stimulus when she had produced that life-saving sneeze, for here the smell of smoke was very strong, an acrid pungent smell that made her already painful eyes water again, made her throat contract sickly. It wasn't just ordinary smoke, either, she realized, but was thick with fumes of some sort, and her weary mind struggled to identify the fumes.

Petrol. It was the heavy smell of partly burned petrol that was making her feel so sick, and now another kind of fear rose in her, and sent her running along the corridor, heedless of the danger of being heard.

'Danny! – Danny!' she called, and her voice came out in a heavy rasping croak that was almost a whisper, so that she tried again, though it hurt her throat abominably to force sounds through it.

'Danny! Where are you? Call again, darling – call again, so that I can find you!' But her voice wouldn't rise above that croaking half whisper, though she felt the veins in her head and neck bulge with the effort she was making.

She threw open each door as she came to it, peering in eagerly, but each room was empty, blank walls and dusty furniture staring back insolently at her, bringing frustration to compound her fear into a paralysing conviction that she and Danny would never leave this house, would stay in it until it burnt away—

For now she could see the smoke as well as smell it, could see it curling in thick lazy tendrils up the main stairwell. And her ears added to the clamour of terror inside her, for she could hear a distant crackling, the sound that is so attractive in fire that is safely confined in a hearth, so redolent of death and disaster when it is uncontrolled, as this crackling was, for it grew perceptibly louder and more eager with each second, as it ate away at the house below her feet.

She turned at the end of the corridor, and stood poised with her back against the window at the end, one part of her screaming 'Get out – get out while you still can—' so that involuntarily she turned and scrabbled at the fastening of the window, aching to get it open, to jump at any risk into the promise of safety in the garden below.

But a stubborn determination came back, made her turn again and stare along the smoke hazed corridor towards the staircase that led upwards.

'Danny,' she whispered huskily. 'I came for him, and I'm going to get him out with me – can't leave him here, can I? You wouldn't want me to leave him here, would you?' And ignoring the insistent little voice inside that screamed with monotonous regularity, 'Get out – get out – get out—' she pushed herself away from the window, and stumbled into the smoke, the smoke that thickened and blurred until she could barely see the stairs at the end.

As she began to go up them, on hands and knees, pulling her desperately heavy body along with aching trembling arms, the crackling noise seemed to diminish a little, giving her new hope. But the smoke was thicker than ever, and suddenly she felt her throat close almost completely, making breathing virtually a physical impossibility.

But she was at the top of the stairs now, and lying flat on the cold polished linoleum. And because she was on a high landing, the smoke was thinner near her head, rising above it to hang heavily ominous against the ceiling above.

It was extraordinary how her memory successively abandoned her and then came to her rescue. She saw another little picture suddenly, herself sitting at a desk in a room full of uniformed nurses, listening to the remote bored voice of a lecturer.

'It is essential,' intoned the voice 'to maintain an air supply in an emergency, and in fires it is possible to trap much of the asphyxiating material in smoke – a mask can be made of any available material—'

She struggled to pull off her jacket, and then ripped off the lace of the little blouse, and wadded it up into a flat pad. With fingers that felt as stiff and useless as a bunch of twigs, she managed to tie the fabric round her nose and mouth, and then, experimentally, took a breath. And it seemed to help, seemed to make the smoke turn away and abandon its efforts to fill her mouth and nose and chest with its acrid poison.

And then she crawled again, forwards, until her head hit a solid surface, until she was against the wall, and could drag herself along it, feeling desperately for a break in the smoothness that might mean a door.

And then she did feel it, the panels, the cool thin movement of air through the crack between jamb and door. And painfully climbed hand over hand until she was kneeling upright with her hand on the knob.

'Danny—' and she didn't know whether she had actually made a sound, or only heard it inside her head.

The doorknob turned uselessly, for even though she leaned against the panels with all her weight it held firm. Again, she let go, and began to slither along the wall in search of yet another door, but stopped, and tried to think logically.

Locked – why locked? None of the doors on the floor below had been locked – and they had been empty. If this one was locked, it must be for a reason. Danny?

She turned her head painfully to look at the door, and realized with a great gush of relief that it wasn't the room into which she herself had been locked, but was directly opposite it. Even in the thickening swirl of grey smoke she could recognize the landing and the arrangement of doors in it – so the locked room *must* be the one for which she was looking.

And she moved back to it, knelt up again, beat on the dumb panels hopelessly, calling 'Danny – Danny' thickly. But no sound came from within, only the distant crackling filling her ears with its triumphant greed as it ate its way into the building below her.

Her hand slithered down helplessly – and was stopped by a sharp pain. The key – the key was in the lock, mutely inviting her to seize it, to turn it. And she tried, so hard, but her aching painful fingers slid away from it, so that she had to use both hands, holding the key with her right hand, and forcing her left to curl its twiggy fingers round it and force the tumblers to fall.

And then the door creaked open, and she fell forwards, into comparatively clean pure air, and visibility.

He was lying in a corner on bare floorboards, for the room was completely bare of any furniture, lying hunched up with his dark curly head pillowed on one crooked arm, looking for all the world as though he had simply fallen into a sweet sleep. And a new strength pulled her to her feet, sent her half-running, half-falling across the room to land on her knees beside him. She put out one hand, taking his shoulder and shaking him gently.

'Danny – Danny, darling – it's me, Abigail – wake up, sweetheart – we've got to get out of here—'

But the child didn't stir, even though she shook him more urgently, even though his head fell back and hit the floor as she moved him.

He was out cold, completely oblivious of what was going on, and as she peered at him, she realized that he wasn't asleep, but deeply unconscious, for his eyes were rolled back, and his mouth lax.

Slight though he was, he was heavy, and for one desperate moment she thought she had been beaten, that the two of them would have to stay where they were to lie curled up together waiting for the greedy flames to crackle nearer and consume them – and the possibility seemed somehow a warm and attractive one. There was an invitation in the thought of lying there in peace and comfort, never to feel pain or terror again.

But the smoke was filling the room now, coming billowing eagerly through the door she had left open, and a deep breath she took unthinkingly made her retch sickly again, banished completely the idea that it would be peaceful and pleasant to die in a fire.

She pulled her mask from her face, and with all the strength she had, ripped it, making two strips of fabric. She folded them, so that the interstices in the heavy cotton lace covered each other, trying to make the masks more effective. One strip she tied over Danny's loose mouth, managing to hold his jaw up with it. Got to maintain an airway. Mustn't let his tongue fall back and choke him, the nurse part of her mind instructed.

Then she tied the remaining mask back over her own face, and bent, and manoeuvred the dead weight of the child's body until his head lay flopping against her back, and his legs dangled helplessly in front of her. Lying like that, said the nurse part of her approvingly, he'll have the added protection of your body against the smoke—

Then, she hooked her own arm round one of his legs and reached behind her for one of his loosely swinging arms. And when she had him in a firm grip in her right hand, she managed to get to her feet, to stand swaying sickly in the centre of the empty attic room – empty but for the heaviness of grey-blue smoke.

It was odd, the way the weight of Danny's inert body balanced her, made it possible for her to walk upright. She moved out of the room, turning awkwardly to get him past the narrow opening. Mustn't scratch him against the wall, she thought absurdly – and using the wall as a guide, moved towards the stairhead.

Getting down was easier than climbing up had been. She hitched Danny forwards slightly, so that his head was against her shoulder rather than the small of her back, and sat down on the top step – and then bumped on her rump awkwardly and childishly, from step to step, down into the house below.

It got hotter as she went down, hotter and thicker, and so much noisier. The crackling had become a busy roaring, a cheering, singing roaring as the fire announced its triumph, and the smoke was lurid with light, rosy rather than grey-blue, rosy and sunny with a warm yellow tinge. Like a September morning, very early, she thought. Pretty. But hotter than September. So much hotter; yet almost pleasant.

She found it easy to stand up once her feet hit the landing, for she just had to lean forwards, and Danny's body slid down her back and balanced her until she was again on her feet, and moving along the wall, using her spare hand to feel her way.

And the second carpeted flight of stairs, was there, miraculously, and again she was sitting on the steps sliding and bumping downwards while Danny's arm slapped heavily against each riser as she moved. But even if it broke his arm, she couldn't do anything about that, and – 'I'm sorry, darling, if I'm hurting you—' she whispered ridiculously.

She could see it then, and found the sight oddly beautiful. Flames were licking gently and languorously round the door frames in the hall below, stretching delicate seeking slender arms across the wall, climbing with swift gaiety up curtains, framing the heavy varnished pictures in fringes of beautiful scarlet and crimson and orange. The light was vivid, but disappeared in sudden heavy clouds of gorgeously coloured smoke, only to reappear again as the smoke rose upwards, filling the stair-well with a cotton woolish loveliness.

And there were other sounds too, loud and clamorous, above the roar and crackling of the flames, sounds that made Abigail feel as though she were at a circus, watching the ring fill with loveliness while she waited with breathless eagerness for lithe and lovely animals to come and leap through the frames of fire that were the doorways.

Shouts and bells and bangs, and louder and louder shouts which rose into a crescendo that made her stop her slow bumping movements down the stairs. For they weren't stairs any more, were they? No, of course they weren't. They were the ranks of seats that surrounded the circus ring, and she and Danny were sitting there, waiting for the clowns and the lovely animals and the trapeze men, and the gorgeous girls perched high on the broad backs of great quiet dignified horses.

And then, beyond the circus ring, the curtains parted. No – not curtains – the big door, the big door with its pretty pieces of blue and red glass in it. Door – or curtains? Of course it must be curtains.

'They always have curtains at circuses, Danny darling,' she whispered in explanation, and sat and stared hopefully at the curtains that looked so like a door. And the opening they framed appeared, widened, and was completely there as the curtains fell with a crash.

'Curtains should go *sideways*, shouldn't they, Danny? Not fall inwards like that—' she said, surprised and somehow annoyed.

And then – 'We've got a gorgeous seat, Danny,' she whispered. 'We can see all the people beyond the curtain – look, darling – can you see? – look—'

But the people didn't stay beyond the curtain, but came pouring through, men in bright heavy brass helmets and heavy black clothes, and as she stared at them stupidly, the circus she had been watching disappeared, and she was back in the house, the house that was blazing around them, and Danny wasn't sitting eager and happy beside her, but was lying helplessly unconscious across her screamingly aching back.

But then he was gone. Someone had lifted him from her, had taken hold of her convulsive grip and gently prised it open and taken him away. And she could see Danny carried out in the arms of a burly man in a big shiny helmet, a man in the shimmering black clothes of a fireman.

She tried to stand up, and swayed and fell forwards. And made no attempt to stop herself, for Danny was safe now, and it just didn't matter, not one bit, whether she fell or not.

But there were arms there, big strong arms, and they caught her and raised her, and something pulled the mask from her face. And then she was moving swiftly, her face pressed against something rough, that smelled good, not smoky or sick or dusty, just *good*.

She was lying on something hard, could feel an incredible coolness on her cheeks, could hear shouts, loud approving shouts, and someone saying 'He'll be all right – get him to the ambulance – they've got oxygen in it – but get well away before you use it – hurry now – and bring up the other ambulance for the other one – move back there – move back.'

She opened her eyes, painfully and stickily, and the thinness of the sunlight after the heavy light of the fire she had been staring at blinded her for a moment.

But then her vision cleared and there was something between her and the sky she was trying to see above it. Fretfully she turned her head, but the something moved too, so that she had to look at it—

A face. A broad craggy face, with dark eyes, staring down at her. A familiar beloved face. And she reached up with one aching hand to touch it, and whispered, 'Oh, where were you? I've wanted you so – and needed you so much, and you weren't there. Darling, darling Miles, where were you?—' and closed her eyes in deep peace as he held her close.

And snapped them open again, and stared at him again and said incredulously 'Max?' And slid at last into the utter peace and comfort of complete oblivion.

CHAPTER TEN

She lay still, cocooned in the warmth of her bed, holding back the moment when awareness would come to flood her with thoughts of the day to come, memories of the yesterday now lost in the past—

But outside things began to creep in, as they always did. There were birds singing somewhere, quite near. And the window must be open wide, for there was a smell of lilac—

Here we go again, said the little voice conversationally. This is where we came in, isn't it?

She opened her eyes, reluctantly, and stared upwards. There was a bottle hanging there, gleaming translucent in the sunshine, a fine tube running from it. Lazily she let her eyes follow it down, past the little glass chamber that let liquid drip rhythmically into a tiny reservoir of sparkling clear fluid, on, until the tube disappeared into a cream coloured bandage. A bandage on her own arm. She looked at it consideringly. A drip. An intravenous drip. How very, very odd.

She moved slightly, and pain shot through her sharply, surprising her into a little whimper. Immediately there was a movement in the room beyond her bed, and she turned her head, painful though it was, and saw him.

'Abigail,' he said, and she smiled at him with a deep delight, with a sense of homecoming and safety that banished the pain in her limbs, made her breathing lose its sharp rasping quality. And extraordinarily, she saw his eyes fill with a sudden brightness that looked like unshed tears.

'Miles – darling, don't look like that—' she said, and

her voice was husky and painful, making that curious sense of startled awareness come again.

'Miles?' she said uncertainly.

'Yes,' he said, and his voice was very soft, but with a warmth in it that was almost tangible, that felt like a balm.

'Can you forgive me, darling? I'll never forgive myself – but if you can, I—' and he shook his head, as though he couldn't say any more.

'Forgive you?' she said, and frowned a little, puzzled. 'What for?'

'Darling – can't you remember yet? I thought – they'd hoped – the doctors – that you would have – you recognized me, you see, *really* recognized me, as myself – and I thought—'

And then it was all there, complete, the edges of the jigsaw puzzle clearly defined, the spaces filled in. She was Abigail Tenterden, and here sitting beside her was her husband. The husband she had forgotten. And now remembered.

Her eyes widened, and she stared at him. 'You *are* Miles. My Miles.'

And his hand closed over her's, big and warm, and he said with a deep relief, 'Yes. Your Miles. Now and—'

'But you were—'

He nodded, his face bleak again. 'Yes. I was Max as well. Can you forgive me for that? It was an abominable thing to have done – but I didn't *know*, you see. Couldn't be sure. And when Danny disappeared it looked so – damning, and I let her tell me— I had to *know*, and that was the only way I could find out. Forgive me, darling. Although I loved you as much as I had from the beginning, I suddenly realized how little I actually *knew* of you. And once before I'd been – wrong, although I hadn't told you that. I'd misled *you* from the start, and

I suppose that was why I was able to believe you were misleading me. And I'll never be able to forget how nearly I lost you because of it, and I'll never be able to forgive myself as long as I live—'

She chuckled softly. 'Heroics, darling, heroics.'

'What?' It was his turn to look startled.

'You're wallowing in heroics and remorse – though I'm still not sure why – the remorse I mean. You'll have to tell me—'

She closed her eyes then, for the lids had become so heavy she couldn't keep them up any longer.

'Soon,' his whisper seemed to come from a long way away. 'I'll tell you soon. But now sleep a while, sweetheart. You need to sleep—'

Momentarily her eyes opened again, and she looked at his blurred figure with its nimbus of light from the window behind him. 'Danny?' she asked, sleepily.

'Doing well, very well. I've seen him, and he's sleeping it all off now, too. You must do the same. I'll explain everything later, I promise.' He put out his hand, and touched her eyelids so that they closed gratefully again.

'Don't go away,' she murmured, pushing back the rising tide of sleep again.

'I won't,' he promised, and she slid blissfully into the tide, let it wash over her, let the ache in her body wash away in it.

And when she woke again, there was no waiting for awareness, for her eyes opened immediately, her head turned to seek him, and he was there, sitting with his shoulders hunched forwards, staring at her with that same considering stare she knew so well. But at the sight of her open eyes, his face cleared, was transformed with a wide warm smile, and his hand tightened over hers.

'Hello,' he said softly.

'Hi, there,' she whispered, and put her face up and he

leaned forwards and kissed her lips very gently, warming her deliciously.

The drip had gone, and she said wonderingly 'When did they take that away?' looking down at her arm with its neat strip of adhesive plaster in the crook of the elbow.

'An hour ago. You were so deeply asleep, you hardly stirred. How do you feel now?'

She moved experimentally. Her body still ached, and breathing was still something she knew was happening, for it hurt to move her chest wall. But the agonizing pain was gone, only a rather pleasant sense of langour remaining.

She smiled up at him. 'I'll live,' she said, and was startled at the response she got, for he lifted her bodily in his arms, and crushed her against him, holding her close and stroking her head with one hand.

And when he released her, she saw, surprised, his face, that craggy heavy face, was streaked with tears. She touched his cheek gently, and said softly 'Not to fret, darling. It's all right now, isn't it? It nearly wasn't, but now it is, so not to fret—'

He lay her back against her pillow, and blew his nose rather noisily. And smiled at her, and said simply 'Yes'.

They stayed there in companionable silence for a long time, Abigail letting her hand rest peaceable in Miles' warm grasp, as she lay and looked at him, just happy to be with him. And then she moved again, and painfully hitched herself up until she was leaning against her pillows in a more upright position.

'Can you tell me, now, what it all was? I can remember quite a lot – all of it, probably, but until you tell me the whole story from the beginning, I won't know if I *have* remembered properly.'

'I'd better make sure you can cope with it all first,' he said, and reached for the bell and rang it.

The nurse that came in was middle aged, and pleasant, and turned Miles out of the room while she 'settled Mrs. Tenterden properly'. Which involved temperature-taking and washing, and manoeuvres with bedpans which amused Abigail quite a bit, for she had never been a hospital patient before, and realized for the first time what it was like to be really bed-fast.

But by the time the nurse had finished, and rung the bell for the ward maid to bring in a tray of hot tea and buttered toast and raspberry jam – 'Tomorrow you can eat more – this is the best thing for this evening—' the nurse said when Abigail made a face and murmured something about real food like bacon and eggs – she felt a good deal more comfortable.

The nurse closed the curtains and turned on the bed-side light, making the room shrink to a pleasing cosiness, and went away to send Miles back.

And he too drank tea from a cup thoughtfully provided by the friendly little ward maid, and watched her as she wolfed her food, and smiled at her, pleased, when she had finished.

'That's made you look a lot better,' he said approvingly. 'Not nearly so peaky—'

'And aching to know everything,' Abigail said. 'I need information now more than I need anything else.'

'Where do I start?'

'At the beginning,' she said. 'Right at the beginning. I've got to match my memories from the time I forgot, you see.'

'Yes—' he swallowed, a little painfully, and said, 'There'll be some things you won't remember, for you never knew about them. You won't like them, I know, but try not to interrupt.'

She grinned a little wickedly. 'That sounds more like

Max than Miles,' and he flushed, and then looked a little rueful as she tightened her hand on his, to take the sting out of her words.

'All right,' he said. 'Here goes. Ten years ago, I married a girl called Constance Cantrell—' she opened her mouth to interrupt, and he put his hand over her lips 'Yes – Cantrell. That was why I chose the name for a pseudonym. It was the one that came into my head at the moment. Well, I – I loved her. Do you mind?' and she smiled and shook her head.

'You love me now, so it doesn't matter,' she said simply, and he raised her hand to his lips and kissed it.

'I loved her,' his voice was stronger now. 'But I soon found out she didn't really care for me. She was more enamoured of the idea of marrying a penniless artist than of me as a person – she was very wealthy, and I – made a change from her usual crew. Well, Daniel was born at the end of our first year of marriage. He – he didn't mean much to me then, really. Babies – well, I knew nothing about them. He was my son, but that was more – more of a *notion* that pleased me. Loving him just wasn't part of the picture. Especially as *she* showed no interest in him. She – she was too busy running about with the various men she'd always run about with.

'Well, when Daniel was still very much a baby, she was killed in a drunken road crash. *And I just didn't care*. I think it was that that upset me most – not caring. I *had* loved her once, you see, at the beginning, but by then – it was dead ashes. And I was glad to be rid of her.'

His face looked grim as he looked back over the years, staring beyond Abigail with a blank gaze. But he seemed to shake himself and went on.

'Daniel had been in the care of his Aunt Cecily from the start. There was nothing to keep me here any more, it seemed to me. A dead and faithless wife, a son who was too young to know or care – so I went away. I took myself to Normandy and I lived there alone for eight years.'

He grinned at her then. 'Odd how it all worked itself out. I wasn't a happy man – but I was a bloody productive one. I've turned out some damned good work these last years.'

He said it without any bragging, but with the calm assurance of the craftsman who is an artist of genius into the bargain, and has the judgement to recognize it.

'I know,' she said softly. 'I've seen a lot of your work. And I can remember how much it mattered to me that you should get well, because of it, when you were assigned to me at the Royal.'

He leaned forwards and kissed her again. 'And saved my life, I think. Anyway, you are just about to enter this story.'

He sat back, and went on in the same considering rather remote voice he had used before.

'It was when Daniel was almost nine that I – remembered I was a father. I had to make some sort of plan for his future, so I unburied myself and came to London to see him.'

He stopped again, and then said painfully, 'It was a shock, meeting him. Such a grave, sensible child. So very much a person. I *liked* him. Extraordinary, really, for he was a stranger to me, after all. And it says a lot for Daniel that he liked me, accepted me as a father, no questions asked, no recriminations at all. Though he'd led an odd and dreary life, it seemed to me, in that huge heavy house, with just Cecily and a couple of servants – and later on, Michael.'

'Michael,' she said. 'I think I remember him. Wasn't he—?'

'You'll hear more about him later,' and Miles' voice hardened. 'Anyway, I had decided to stay in England, to start being a real father for Daniel, when I let myself get run over.'

He sounded disgusted. 'Christ, but it was stupid. I walked across Oxford Street as though it were the village street at Moulins Verts – and got myself mixed up with a taxi. It was worth it though, because that was how I found you.'

He smiled at her then, and said softly, 'Do you remember?'

She nodded. She remembered very well. The way she had felt when Sister Bartlett had said 'We've got a new patient – road accident. Head injuries, for observation. You'd better take him—' The way his name had made her jerk into anxiety, fearful that so blazing a talent should be snuffed out. The way he had looked during the early worrying days of his recovery, how helplessly she had fallen in love with him. And the heaven of finding he loved her too. The whirlwind of their growing relationship, and the way they lived in a daze of happiness. Their wedding, with just two of her friends from the Royal there. The solemn way Daniel had shaken hands with her when Miles had said simply, 'This is Abigail. I hope you two can like each other.' The way he had looked at her with a considering gaze that turned her heart over, so like Miles' was it, and said 'I think I shall like her. She has an open face, not a shut-up one like Auntie Cissie's—' Yes, she remembered very well.

Miles settled back in his chair again, and went on talking. 'I suppose I should have realized it might happen – but I was too besotted with love, too deep in bliss at being alive again, with you, to think of anything or anyone. We moved into the house with Cecily and Daniel, and I never thought about how she might be feeling—'

'She was very kind to me, you know,' Abigail said.

'But I – I never felt I knew her. We were always just – polite acquaintances, you know? But I didn't care either. There was you, and there was Daniel – it was all so wonderful—'

'Yes,' he said soberly. 'And all the time Cecily was eaten up with hate for us both. And her feeling for Daniel – that turned itself inside out too. I know now – I can see it all, with hindsight. And I've talked to that bastard Michael, too, and got a good deal out of him. They saved him, you see. She – didn't make it.'

She stared at him, suddenly alarmed 'Cecily?'

He nodded. 'She died in the fire, darling.'

Abigail closed her eyes in sick horror, and his voice came from a long way away. 'Darling – I'm sorry – have I upset you? Please, don't. The firemen say she couldn't have felt pain – it was the smoke that killed her. She was dead before – before the fire took complete hold and gutted the house.'

She opened her eyes. 'Go on,' she said drearily. 'Go on explaining.'

'Well, Cecily developed a hate for both of us – because Daniel who'd always been *hers*, like some piece of property, in his childlike way made no attempt to hide his preference for us. He turned away from her completely – not that he'd ever cared that much for her, but she didn't realize this. She saw us as thieves of his affection. And hated him for being so atttached to us. And there was something else.'

'What more could there be?'

'Money,' he said succinctly. 'Daniel is a rich little boy. His mother left all her money to him – and Cecily never really forgave Constance for that. The money had been their father's and he'd left his house property to Cecily, but the cash to Constance. And when Constance died, Cecily thought the money should have reverted to her, but she accepted Daniel as the inheritor since I so obligingly handed him over to her. But you can imagine how she felt when I came back – with a lovely girl like you in tow – making it clear that Daniel was my son, and would leave Cecily eventually, taking his inheritance with him.'

Miles looked sick suddenly, and then said awkwardly. 'And there was one other factor in this whole sick and sorry mess – which I, in my arrogance and self-centred happiness, completely forgot. Constance was the sister I'd married – but Cecily was the one who loved me. I – I knew that, but I thought – as men do – that she'd get over it. But apparently she never did. She always hoped I'd come back one day and marry her. Instead of which I came back and married – you.'

'I can't blame her,' Abigail said softly. 'Poor Cecily.'

'Poor stupid Cecily – for loving me *was* stupid, wasn't it? Anyway, this is where Michael comes in. I know Cecily was somewhat faded and looked older than her age when you met her for the first time, but she wasn't forty – only two or three years older than me. And she had been attractive once.'

Abigail nodded. 'I think – I can imagine that. If she hadn't looked so – petulant, I think it was, she could have been much nicer to look at. But what about Michael?'

'I don't know where she found him, but he came to work as general factotum at the house. And developed a big thing for Cecily. I think it was partly genuine – not entirely a self-seeking attempt to get money out of an obviously well-off woman. She had quite a lot in her own right you see, for there was the other house property she owned and earned rents from, and of course she had full use of Daniel's income. She may have seemed richer than she was. Anyway Michael fell for her, not her money, though I daresay it helped push him into feeling as he did.'

'I hardly ever saw him,' Abigail said, memory glazing her eyes as she stared back into those months following her marriage. 'He was always slithering out of sight when I got a glimpse of him. And though Cecily said she'd take a back seat and let me run things, as a married woman, I didn't want to. I was happy to let her run the house and leave me just to be with you, watching you work, or being with Daniel. But she was – she tried to be nice to me, didn't she, Miles? The way she let me decide about the repainting of the house. I remember that. And it was *her* house, after all.'

'Feeding the flames, that was,' Miles said, and at her puzzled look added, 'Encouraging you to usurp her place, as she saw it, even more – so that she could hate you more virulently and with more just cause. I should have realized, I suppose, should have warned you, but I didn't think. I'd told you nothing of the past – just that I'd been married once. That was all. You knew nothing of the tangle of the relationships, and in a stupid attempt to keep myself – honourable – in your eyes, I misled you. Forgive me, if you can—'

'Of course I can. And I never thought about your past marriage because it was irrelevant to me. I mean, I assumed you'd once loved Constance too much to talk about it at all. And as long as you loved me now nothing else mattered—'

'And I do love you now – very much, my darling,' he said, and kissed her again.

The door of the room opened sharply and the nurse came in, smiling benevolently at the way they jumped and sprang apart.

'Obviously feeling much better, Mrs. Tenterden,' she said, and laughed at Abigail's sudden blush. 'But enough is enough. Sleep, now. You've had a stormy passage, you know, and you can't keep on improving like this without plenty of rest. Your husband can come back in the morning—'

And Abigail, with the story still half told, had to let Miles go and submit to sleep even though she was sure she couldn't rest without knowing the whole story.

But the nurse put out the light firmly, and left her to the silence and the little voice deep in her own mind.

What do you suppose, she asked it, what do you suppose Michael—

But not only did she not get an answer. She didn't finish the question. She fell abruptly and deeply asleep before she could complete it.

CHAPTER ELEVEN

They let her get out of bed the next morning, after the doctor had come to see her and looked complacent about the way she had improved.

'A few days here, and then a good long holiday, and you'll be like new again,' he said. 'Daniel? No, not yet, my dear. He needs time to rest, too. He's been damaged more in a psychological sense than a physical one, so he'll need time to get over things. Make haste slowly, my dear, make haste slowly.' And he nodded and went away.

And when Miles came, bearing a huge sheaf of spring flowers to fill her room with a drift of narcissus and daffodils and mimosa, she was sitting in an armchair, rug enveloped, and looking far more like the person she remembered as herself. And he kissed her lingeringly, and sat beside her with one of her hands cradled in both of his.

'Tell me the rest of it, Miles,' she said. 'Once we've got it all straight and out of our systems, we can forget all about it, and start new. Can't we?'

'Yes,' he said, and kissed her again. 'Well, you've got all the background clear now. So all that's left is what happened as a – climax to it. I've got it all pretty clear, now—'

'I'm listening,' she said, and settled herself more comfortably.

'I had to go back to Normandy to settle things there – sell my cottage, arrange to ship my canvases home—'

'I remember!' she said eagerly. 'And I missed you horribly, and suddenly thought of trying to buy a present for you, because you'd given me so much, and I – I'd given you nothing.'

'Nothing? Oh, Abigail, if only you knew—' he said, and she shook her head.

'You know what I mean. And I bought that cottage near Cirencester with the money Daddy left me—'

'And told me nothing about it in your letters.'

'It was to be a surprise.'

'It was certainly that,' he said grimly. 'Anyway, this is what happened, as far as I can work it out. Cecily started to talk to you – to hint things about me—'

She nodded, her face clouding. 'Yes. She – she told me you didn't care about Daniel at all – only wanted his money. Oh, I didn't *believe* her – at least I didn't think I did—'

'But poison like that leaves a mark – of course it does. She did the same thing to me. Wrote and hinted that you – you were— Oh, God, I'm sorry to say this, darling, but she made me suspect you were having an affair with Michael. And I knew so little of you, you see, only that I'd fallen head over ears in love with you—'

'I was in the same boat,' she whispered. 'She – she had a way of saying things that made them stick in one's mind, like – like a broken tooth. You know it hurts, yet you keep exploring it with your tongue—'

'Exactly. Anyway, as far as I understand it, she came to you one night and said—'

'I can tell *you*,' Abigail cut in. 'She came to my room, just as I'd finished writing a letter, to you, and said you were in the house. That you'd come back unexpectedly and secretly, and were downstairs. That she'd heard you come to Daniel's door, and call him out, and take him downstairs with you – and that she was afraid you were – were going to hurt him in some way. That if Daniel died, you'd be rich – and – and—'

121

'And you went downstairs to see—'

'I didn't believe her, darling – not really. But I went into the drawing room, and the – the mess was awful. Furniture pushed out of place, and – and Daniel lying there—'

'It was Michael, you see,' Miles said. 'He was very deeply involved with Cecily. They'd planned the whole thing. He was to – to kill Danny, and you, and then incriminate me. That would get rid of all three of us. They sent me a telegram – Cecily did. Said you'd gone away with Michael.' He shivered. 'The journey home was sheer *hell*. I didn't believe it, you see, but I wondered – couldn't help wondering.'

'Look, Miles – let's clear one thing up here and now. No recriminations, no guilt about what we were both led to believe. All right? We were manipulated – and we couldn't help it. Is that a deal?'

'I love you,' he said simply, and bent his head to kiss her again. 'Fair enough. No recriminations – as if I could – and no guilt – if I can prevent myself from feeling it, which is doubtful.

'Now, to sort things out more clearly. It was *Michael* who'd beaten up poor Danny. But thank God he was an inefficient murderer, because he didn't succeed in killing him, *or* you. It was he who knocked you out as you bent over Danny—'

She nodded, bleakly. 'It all makes sense now. I woke up, I remember – I felt dreadful, but Danny was stirring, and I knew I had to get him away to safety, somehow. I – I thought it *had* been you who'd tried to kill us – I'm – sorry, darling—'

'No guilt, no recriminations. Remember?'

'No guilt. All right. I thought it was you, then, and that you would come back and – and finish the job. So I had to get away with Danny. I was too – confused,

I suppose, to do the sensible thing. Or still loved you too much. Anyway, I *didn't* go to the police. I wrapped Danny in a blanket, and went and grabbed some clothes – I don't know where Cecily was—'

'She and Michael left the house – to establish an alibi, I gather that was the idea,' Miles said.

'I was so frightened,' she said, painfully dredging up the memory. 'So frightened. But I got out of the house with Danny, carrying him like a baby, and took him in a taxi to Paddington, and got on a train to Cirencester. It was the only place I could think of – I was so glad I'd managed to keep the fact I'd bought the cottage a secret. And when we got there, Danny was fairly fit. He seemed to have recovered from his walloping pretty well. Children do, don't they?'

'Anyway, I then realized we couldn't hide there for ever, in the cottage. We'd have to come out some time. But I was so past things, then. So worn out I couldn't think straight. I remember telling Danny I had to go out for a while – I think I *was* going to the police. I left him with some sandwiches and milk I'd bought on the way, and I can remember walking down the path in the morning light – the sun was shining right in my eyes, so I couldn't see, and – and—'

She struggled to remember, but then shook her head. 'And then I woke up in that hotel bedroom.'

'I think that was when the amnesia really hit you. The doctor said there'd still be some gaps, and it seems he's right. I can fill in a bit now, anyway.

'I got to the house late the same night it all happened. I was *supposed* to find two – dead bodies and then the police would think I'd killed you. No one else in the house, you see. And Cecily was to deny ever sending me a telegram. All I found was the drawing room looking like – like an abattoir, almost. Obviously something grim had

123

happened. I nearly went mad. Searched the house, but there was no one there – and then Cecily and Michael came in. She said she'd been to a theatre, and Michael had gone with her to be chauffeur, and she'd treated him to the play as well. They both looked thunderstruck when they saw the drawing room, I remember. I thought it was because of the mess, but of course it was because you two weren't there – stupid conspirators, weren't they? Thank God for it – their not making sure you were both – dead—'

'It's quite difficult to kill people. Difficult to recognize death, too. I know *that* for certain.'

'It was I who called the police,' Miles said soberly. 'And the fuss and the questioning – it was hell. And when they'd finished with us it was the middle of the night. But I had to do something – couldn't just sit there gnawing my heart out. So I started doing some – detecting – myself. I took the car and went to every mainline station there was – I couldn't bring myself to believe you were bad, though the police clearly thought you had killed Danny, and gone off with – with his body, after they'd finished talking to Cecily, and she'd told them her version of your behaviour – which was that you'd lost interest in Michael and gone off with some other man. And Michael, rot his soul, said the same thing.

'But I couldn't believe it. So I went out asking – and at Paddington I found someone who remembered you – the man who sold you your ticket. He remembered a frantic girl with a child wrapped in a blanket, buying tickets to Cirencester. So I took the car and followed you. And looked at every hotel register until I struck oil. Your handwriting, and Mrs. Miles – it was all I needed.'

'And when I came down next day and saw you—'

He looked embarrassed. 'I – I thought it was an act on your part – a brilliant act, but an act all the same. And on the spur of the moment, invented the journalist Max Cantrell. I had to, you see. I *had* to. I couldn't think of any other way to play it. If you *were* acting, you'd have to accept me, to avoid giving yourself away. If it were true – that you'd lost your memory – well, it was the only way to find out what had happened to Danny. I realized very quickly it was real – your amnesia. And didn't dare give up my – alias, in case I shocked you into an even deeper amnesia. And the rest, you know—'

'Not quite. Why did Michael follow me to Cirencester, too? He saw me across the square, you see – it *was* him. How did he know where to—'

'Did what I did,' Miles said crisply. 'Asked at railway stations till he picked up the trail. It wasn't difficult. Not many distraught girls carrying largish children buy railway tickets at that hour of the night, and then have equally frantic men asking questions about them. He found us easily. I imagine he too wanted to know where Danny was – he won't say why he followed us, but it seems pretty obvious. He still wanted to kill you and Danny, and frame me. Then, and only then, would Cecily inherit, and he share the results. Because he had every intention of marrying her.'

'And what about that Inspector – did *he* follow us too, in the same way?'

'No. You were right, up to a point. He *was* a CID man. I'd told them what was up before I left town. And deeply regretted it once I'd caught up with you. I was trying to persuade him you'd gone back to London, when you overheard us. I think he *must* have believed it eventually, even after you shot off as you did. He turned up at the London house just before I got you out—'

'Darling,' Abigail said, with sudden contrition. 'What *did* happen when I shot off after Michael, from that café, and left you? I had to do it – I'm sorrier than I can say—'

He laughed then. 'God, but that was hell. As I walked into the café, I realized the man had just left – I had no idea who he was – for a while I'd even suspected he was a – a figment of your imagination. But I got out in time to see the two of you drive out – and got a glimpse of Michael, and realized the danger. The whole thing suddenly made *sense*. I was frantic – nearly went mad with fear for you, in case he spotted you, and got at you. It took me more than an hour to get at the police, and convince them of the danger – but then we followed you, two burly coppers and me in a screaming police car. And got to the house too late to stop you going in. The traffic – the early morning rush-hour – was so thick that in spite of that screeching siren we were held up all the way. And when we got there, the fire engines were out and the house was blazing– and I saw the car parked by the square, and I – I think I died a little in that moment,' he finished simply.

She put up her arms, and held him close. 'But you got there. That's what really matters—'

'I got there,' he said against her hair. 'And you, you bloody marvellous woman, got that child out. You're more than a heroine, my angel. You're – I don't know a word that could describe you. You got that child out of the fire Cecily and Michael started – to finish their horrible job. Dear Abigail, have I told you how much I love you?'

'No,' she whispered. 'Not nearly often enough. Tell me again.'

And he did, for about half an hour, until the arrival of a nurse with a cup of chocolate for each of them, and strict instructions that Mrs. Tenterden was to return to bed forthwith, pulled them reluctantly apart.

And later, the chocolate warm inside her, lying warm

and relaxed in bed again, surprised to discover how grateful she was to be there, she looked up at him, again sitting beside her, and grinned a little wickedly, holding his hand against her cheek.

'Darling Miles,' she said. 'Do you know something?'

'Mmm?' He smiled down at her with his eyes crinkled into a warmth that made her feel as safe and protected as a baby.

'I'm awfully glad you decided to be Max Cantrell.'

'Why? Was he a nicer bloke than Miles Tenterden?'

'No,' and she turned her face and kissed his fingers. 'Because it's so marvellous falling in love. And I did it *twice* – with the same man. So lovely and *respectable* to fall in love with a stranger who's your husband – almost worth nearly being murdered for.'

She yawned suddenly and hugely.

'Almost worth it – but not quite' and put her arms round her husband and kissed him in a very wifely manner indeed.